KISSING RACHEL

"You know, I have always thought of you as a woman of sunshine, so bright and warm with life, but you appear quite provocative by the light of the moon."

Rachel's breath became unsteady as she met the smoldering dark gaze.

"Why, Anthony, was that a compliment?"

"merely an observation. I leave empty compliments to rogues and schoolboys."

She stepped closer, her heart thundering in her chest. "Do you have any other observations?"

He smiled as his hands moved from her shoulders to trail his fingers along the line of her plunging neckline.

"I suppose that I could tell you that your skin possesses the purity of a rare pearl and that your eyes have been kissed with gold dust. Or that your lips are perfectly formed to fit my own."

"Oh."

Clearly sensing her rising passion Anthony slowly lowered his head to claim her lips in a branding kiss.

Rachel melted against him, her hands stroking over the firm muscles of his chest. For the moment it did not matter what magic he possessed that set her body ablaze. She only knew that she wished to discover where these tumultuous sensations would lead. . . .

Books by Debbie Raleigh

LORD CARLTON'S COURTSHIP

LORD MUMFORD'S MINX

A BRIDE FOR LORD CHALLMOND

A BRIDE FOR LORD WICKTON

A BRIDE FOR LORD BRASLEIGH

THE CHRISTMAS WISH

THE VALENTINE WISH

THE WEDDING WISH

Published by Zebra Books

THE WEDDING
WISH

Debbie Raleigh

ZEBRA BOOKS
Kensington Publishing Corp.
http://www.kensingtonbooks.com

ZEBRA BOOKS are published by

Kensington Publishing Corp.
850 Third Avenue
New York, NY 10022

All Kensington titles, imprints, and distributed lines are
available at special quantity discounts for bulk purchases for
sales promotion, premiums, fund-raising, educational or in-
stitutional use.

Special book excerpts or customized printings can also be
created to fit specific needs. For details, write or phone the
office of the Kensington Special Sales Manager: Kensington
Publishing Corp., 850 Third Avenue, New York, NY 10022.
Attn. Special Sales Department. Phone: 1-800-221-2647.

First Printing: April 2002
10 9 8 7 6 5 4 3 2 1

Printed in the United States of America

One

The lush, opulent beauty of the Opera house went largely unappreciated by the vast crowds that moved through the corridors and flitted from box to box. The vast crowds did not attend the opera to marvel at the glittering beauty of the surroundings or the extravagant performance being enacted upon the stage. One quite simply went to the opera to see and be seen.

Standing near the grand staircase Miss Rachel Cresswell watched the passing throng with a lively interest. Although it was still February, a number of the ton had grown weary of the harsh winter and had fled back to the pleasures of London.

At first glance she was a pretty maiden. Her form was tiny, but nicely curved, her hair the shade of ripe wheat and her hazel eyes sprinkled with gold. But it was not her dainty features or porcelain skin that had ensured that she would be toasted as an Incomparable throughout every gentleman's club in London.

It was instead the vibrant energy that shimmered and swirled about her. This was no insipid debutant, the gentlemen universally agreed. She was bold, reckless, and daringly alive. She was also maddeningly elusive. A mixture designed to capture the attention of the most jaded rogue.

Well aware of her fatal allure, Rachel accepted her bevy of admirers with careless satisfaction. And why not? As the daughter of the Devilish Dandy she knew that the doors to society should have been firmly closed against her. There was an ironic sense of justice in forcing the thin-lipped, disapproving hostesses to issue her invitations or risk an uprising by their male guests.

Attired in a satin gown in a daring shade of burgundy, Rachel slowly waved her fan against the oppressive heat. At her side a tall, sinfully attractive gentleman gazed longingly at the provocative cut of her neckline.

"You are exquisite," he was whispering in a tone he had perfected to send a thrill down a lady's spine. "As beautiful as a sunrise, as tempting as . . ."

"Really, Mr. Mondale, you are becoming repetitive," Rachel drawled, supremely indifferent to the fact this gentleman was considered irresistible by most females. "You compared me to a sunrise only last evening."

The deep blue eyes sparkled with amusement. "It is only because words are such a paltry means of revealing the depth of my desire for you, my dove. There are far more pleasurable methods of proving such sweet emotions."

"No doubt." Rachel lifted a hand to stifle a yawn.

Mr. Mondale gave an appreciative chuckle even as he moved closer to savor the faint scent of roses that clung to her skin.

"How long do you intend to torment me?" he asked.

"For as long as you amuse me."

"Devil."

Rachel sighed. "And only moments ago I was an angel fallen from heaven."

"Let us leave this place. I must be alone with you."

"Do not be absurd." Rachel paid little heed to the predictable attempts at seduction; instead her restless gaze abruptly landed on a dark male form standing across the corridor. She was uncertain what had captured her attention. He was handsome enough, she conceded, in a rather poetic manner. His dark hair was longer than fashionable and his features finely chiseled. But his black attire was without adornment and his presence unassuming. He should have been easily overlooked, and yet she discovered herself oddly intrigued by the stillness settled about his lean form and the compelling intensity in the black eyes. He was so very different from the other flamboyant dandies parading through the crowd. "Who is that?"

Careful to disguise any hint of impatience at her pointed lack of regard for his determined pursuit, Mr. Mondale turned to scan the crowd.

"Where?"

"The gentleman attired in black."

"Ah, Anthony Clarke."

"I do not believe I have ever seen him about."

Mr. Mondale shrugged. "I should be surprised if you had. He is an inventor and doesn't much care for society. Prefers to dabble with gadgets and whatnots than making a dash in town."

"He prefers gadgets to society?" she demanded in disbelief. "He must be very odd."

"Peculiar perhaps, but a nice-enough chap."

Rachel's gaze traveled over the dark form. Despite her certainty that anyone who would willingly seclude themselves from society must be a bit daft, she could not deny a hint of curiosity about Anthony Clarke.

"He does have beautiful eyes," she murmured. "And very nice shoulders."

"A waste of your talent, my princess," Mr. Mondale mocked lightly.

She gave a cool lift of her brows. "Pardon me?"

"Clarke will never be bewitched by a mere female, even one as lovely as you."

"Why do you say that?"

"The gentleman is one of the richest in England. He has had every debutant, widow, and courtesan tossing themselves at his feet since he came of age. No matter how eligible or how beautiful, they have never managed to stir the faintest hint of interest. Only the exquisite Pandora has ever managed to claim a small part of his life, and that is simply because she is as cold-blooded as himself."

Rachel's eyes narrowed in a predatory manner. She was a female accustomed to all too easy conquests. The thought that there might be a gentleman indifferent to her charms was bound to pique her interest.

"A challenge."

"Fah." Mr. Mondale attempted to distract her wandering attention. "The man has ice in his veins. He could never appreciate a vibrant, passionate woman. I, on the other hand, am capable of full, unbridled appreciation. Would you desire me to demonstrate?"

She flashed him a speaking glance. "You have demonstrated quite enough, Mr. Mondale."

"I have only begun," he warned in fervent tones, leaning forward to blow softly in her ear. Then, noting the slender boyishly handsome gentleman approaching them with an eager expression, he stiffened. "Damnation. It appears that one of your bevy of love-struck schoolboys is about to descend upon us."

Slowly turning, Rachel allowed a small smile to curve her lips. Mr. Mondale was not to know that Lord Newell was not just another admirer. She had taken special care to ensnare the young gentleman the moment he had arrived in London.

Now she willingly held out her hand and allowed the gentleman to press a fervent kiss upon her fingers.

"Miss Cresswell," he breathed with a charming innocence. "I feared I might not discover you among this dreadful crush."

Rachel pulled her hand free as she glanced coyly through her tangle of thick, black lashes. "Surely, my lord, you have not been searching for me?"

He appeared shocked that she would even have to ask. "But of course I have. I never would have allowed myself to be bullied into coming to such a devilishly dull place if it weren't for the hope of meeting you. As it is I was forced to endure a near hour of that wretched screeching before I could slip from the box."

"Gads, the boy still smells of the nursery," Mr. Mondale whispered in her ear. "Let us be gone from here."

Rachel ignored the rogue at her side and instead directed the full impact of her charm upon the hapless Lord Newell.

"How very dreadful for you, my lord."

"I say," Lord Newell agreed morosely, then his expression abruptly brightened. "Still, it was worth every moment to see you."

"What a charming thing to say."

"It is only the truth. You must know how I feel."

"Do I?" she coaxed softly.

On the point of swearing his undying devotion, Lord Newell was halted as a large matron attired in a hideous yellow silk stepped into the corridor and stabbed him with a steely gaze.

"George," she called loudly, her long face pinched with fury at the sight of the young lord paying obvious court to Rachel.

"Dash it all," Lord Newell muttered, his countenance flaming with embarrassment.

"Is there a problem, my lord?" Rachel demanded in lazy amusement.

"My godmother. She is determined to leg-shackle me to that whey-faced daughter of hers."

Rachel's gaze moved to the two maidens standing behind Lady Broswell. They bore an unfortunate resemblance to their mother, with their long, pale faces and broad forms. A secretive smile curved her lips.

"How very unfortunate."

"A bloody nuisance," Lord Newell mourned.

"George," Lady Broswell shrilly called again, her face an ugly shade of crimson. "Come away at this moment. How dare you consort with a common tart?"

"My lady," Lord Newell protested in shock.

Rachel snapped shut her fan, the hazel eyes glittering with a dangerous fire.

"A tart?" she demanded in silky tones.

"What could one expect from the daughter of a notorious thief?" Lady Broswell spat, too angry to note the gathering crowd. "Everyone knows that your father is fit for nothing more than a hangman's noose."

"At least my father taught me a measure of good manners," Rachel gritted. "It appears to be sadly lacking in some members of society."

"You are a spawn of the devil and I can only thank

goodness we shall be leaving for Surrey tomorrow where those such as you are not welcome."

"I am certain London will celebrate your absence."

Somewhere in the crowd someone giggled at the thrust and the long face quivered with rage.

"Why you ill-bred jade. I suppose I should expect no better from you."

"Really? And why is that?" Rachel drawled

"Blood always runs true," Lady Broswell retorted in angry arrogance.

"Ah, you wish to speak of bloodlines?" Rachel demanded with a cold smile.

Genuine fear flashed in the older woman's eyes as she belatedly realized her mistake. As a rule she was very cautious to hide her attempts to bar Rachel from polite society behind closed doors. She far preferred malicious rumors to direct confrontation. After all, there was always the knowledge she might provoke Rachel into revealing the truth about them.

Now she wet her thin lips as she sought a means of escape without appearing a coward.

"George, we are leaving. I will not have my daughters exposed to such a woman."

"But, my lady . . ." Lord Newell stuttered.

"Now, George."

She surged past Rachel and down the staircase like a battleship in full retreat.

"Forgive me," Lord Newell muttered, acutely embarrassed as he offered her a hasty bow. "I shall call upon you the moment I return from Surrey."

Keeping a smile pasted on her stiff lips, Rachel turned back to her companion as the boy hurried in the wake of his godmother. She had never been so furious in her life. How dare the harridan insult her in such a public manner? To call her a tart and the spawn of the devil . . . and then, to imply her precious daughters might be sullied by her mere presence . . . it all went beyond the pale.

She longed to launch herself at the retreating matron. To force her to admit they had far more in common than she wished to acknowledge.

Instead she calmly waved her fan as her fingers unconsciously toyed with the large ruby hung about her neck. She was painfully aware of the large crowd that had gathered to witness the ugly scene. She was not about to provide the avid gossip-seekers with grist for their mills. The only means of enduring a public humiliation was to pretend that it had never occurred.

"Gads, what a surly old witch," Mr. Mondale murmured, his gaze studying her far too bright eyes. "She does not appear to care much for you, my dove."

"This time she has pressed me too far," Rachel swore between gritted teeth.

"I do not particularly care for that expression on you lovely features. What are you plotting?"

Rachel gave a start of surprise. She was indeed plotting, but she had not expected the rogue to be so perceptive. She was clearly in need of privacy to complete the details of her burning desire for revenge.

"Nothing more scandalous than a visit to Surrey," she retorted in flippant tones.

"Surrey?" Mr. Mondale gave a shudder of disgust. "You must be jesting. You would be bored witless within a day."

"Actually, I can think of few things more entertaining at the moment," she assured him in dangerously soft tones. "Now if you will excuse me, I must be on my way."

With her head held high Rachel swept through the crowd and down the staircase. She knew that there were a wave of twitters behind her, but her expression remained regally serene as she collected her cloak and moved to await the Amberly carriage that had brought her to the opera along with Mrs. Amberly and her daughter Serena. Mrs. Amberly was unlikely to desire to leave the performance early, Rachel was certain. There would be ample time to be taken to the small home she shared with her father and have the carriage returned to collect her hostess. She would tell a servant to inform Mrs. Amberly that she had developed a headache and was forced to seek the comfort of her bed.

Allowing a footman to settle the fur-lined cloak about her shoulders, Rachel impatiently turned to pace across the shadowed foyer. "Lady Broswell desire a battle," she muttered beneath her breath. Well, she was quite happy to provide her with one. Miss Rachel Cresswell had never backed down from a challenge in her life.

Intent on her dark thoughts, Rachel did not realize she was no longer alone. Not until she abruptly turned about and collided sharply with a firm male body.

"Oh."

"Careful," a dark, smoky voice murmured as a pair of strong arms encircled her waist to keep her upright.

A pleasurable shiver raced through Rachel as she instinctively realized she was pressed next to the mysterious Mr. Clarke. Just for a moment she allowed her hand to rest upon the contoured muscles of his chest, the male heat swirling about her. Then slowly she tilted back her head to meet the black gaze, unprepared for the strange jolt of awareness that had her hastily stepping back.

She was uncertain what had just occurred. Over

the past few years she had encountered countless gentlemen. Some charming, some witty, and some wickedly dangerous. But none had actually managed to flutter her heart until now.

Telling herself that she was being ridiculous, Rachel summoned an apologetic smile.

"Forgive me. I fear that I was not paying proper heed to where I was going."

Expecting the usual expression of dazzled delight, she was intrigued when the dark gaze merely made a lazy survey of her perfect features.

"Understandable under the circumstances."

She gave a rueful grimace. "You witnessed that horrid scene?"

"Difficult not to."

"Yes, I suppose. I possess a dreadful temper."

A faint smile touched the generously carved lips. "I believe that you were suitably provoked."

Provoked? Rachel clenched her hands beneath the cloak. Lady Broswell had thrown down the gauntlet. Clearly she hoped Rachel was too cowardly to accept her challenge.

"That harridan," she muttered. "I shall make her sorry."

"Ah, I thought as much. Miss Cresswell, may I offer you a warning?"

She met the deep black gaze with a small frown, barely noting the fact that he obviously knew her identity. "What do you mean?"

"The path of revenge is rarely fulfilling. You would be better served forgetting Lady Broswell's insults."

"Not on this occasion. It is high time the woman learned a lesson in common manners."

Slender fingers reached up to softly stroke her heated cheek. "Such a b—beautiful lady should be enjoying her life, not dwelling upon retribution for meaningless slights."

Delighted by the sensations of his gentle touch, she gazed at him in surprise.

"You have a stutter."

"Yes, I have noticed," he said in dry tones.

"Oh, I am sorry."

His hand dropped as he gave a vague shrug. "F—for what? You spoke nothing but the truth."

"I think it is charming," Rachel informed him sincerely. There was something very enticing about that low, smoky voice, even with its faint stutter.

He gave a low chuckle at her artless words. "You are a delicious minx and far too aware of your own powers, my dear." His hand once again rose to trace the outline of her lips. Rachel's heart shuddered at the brief caress. "But have a care. I should not like to see you hurt by the flames of your own passions."

Perhaps for the first time in her life Rachel felt that she was out of her depth. Always before she had set out her lures and calmly watched as her prey entangled themselves. It was a game she had played on a hundred occasions. Now, she wondered who precisely was the prey.

Her thoughts were disturbed as a footman stepped into the foyer. The carriage had arrived and she suddenly realized that she did not wish this moment to end. What if she never saw him again?

"Mr. Clarke?" she said urgently.

"Yes?"

"I should like to see your inventions someday."

He smiled, but his expression was inscrutable. "Perhaps."

She bit her lip, not at all satisfied with his vague response. Was it possible that he did not feel the same tingling excitement that she did? The thought was rather sobering. And more than a little provoking.

Still, with the footman hovering at her side she could do nothing more than sweep an elegant curtsy and follow the servant to the waiting carriage.

She should be considering how best to carry out her revenge, she chided herself as she stepped into the chilled February night. It was no time to be distracted by a pair of midnight eyes and a voice of smoke.

Even if he did send chills down her spine.

Anthony Clarke remained in the shadows as the bewitching Miss Cresswell swept from the foyer.

A smile curved his lips.

He had not wanted to come to the opera this evening. Indeed, it had only been a direct command from his great-aunt that had prodded him to make a reluctant appearance among society. Now he realized he owned the old tartar his gratitude.

It had been far too long since he had experienced the sharp thrill of desire, he acknowledged. For the past few years he had devoted his attention to his various inventions. Not only was he fascinated by the process of using his hands to create the ideas that hovered in the back of his mind, but it provided a welcome distraction from the aimless social rounds and gaming hells that dominated the lives of most gentlemen in his position. It also kept him too occupied to be plagued by the endless fortune hunters who had hovered about him like vultures since coming to London.

Perhaps he had been a bit too determined to avoid society, he admitted with a tingle of anticipation. Although he had heard rumors of the dashing Miss

Cresswell, and of course, her father who was a wanted criminal, he had never expected her to be quite so intriguing.

Certainly she was a minx with a brash confidence in her potent charm. But there was also a hint of sweet vulnerability in the depths of those magnificent hazel eyes. And a wild passion that would tempt a saint.

Yes, indeed, it was obvious he would have to put aside his inventions for the moment.

It was high time he indulged a few of his less intellectual senses.

"There you are, Anthony," an impatient voice broke into his musings. "What are you doing skulking in the shadows?"

Turning his head, Anthony regarded his cousin, Lord Varnwell, with a half smile. As always the young dandy was attired in a painfully bright waistcoat with a cravat that threatened to engulf half his face. Anthony had attempted to instill a trace of restraint in his relative's unfortunate choice in fashion, but his efforts had thus far proved to be sadly ineffective.

Still, Varnwell was a pleasant, if trifle stupid young man and Anthony was fond of him.

"You would b—be amazed what you can discover in the shadows."

A sly expression settled upon the youthful features. "Such as the delectable Miss Cresswell?"

Anthony crossed his arms over his chest. "She is delectable."

"Egads, do not tell me that you have at last encountered a female who can stir that cold heart?" Lord Varnwell teased.

"Just because I allow myself to be led by logic

rather than lust does not mean I possess a cold heart."

"I do not think you were pondering logic when you were flirting with the Cresswell wench."

Anthony recalled the raw heat that had flared through him when Miss Cresswell had slammed into his arms. He slowly smiled. It was a heat he was anxious to rekindle.

"N—not entirely."

"Perhaps you will have more luck than the rest of us in bedding the chit." Lord Varnwell sighed, blithely unaware of the tightening of his cousin's mouth. "She has proved to be annoyingly elusive, but I doubt even she could resist your scandalous fortune."

"Must you be so crude?" Anthony snapped, uncertain whether he was angered at the insult to Miss Cresswell or the implication that his only attraction lay in a nearby bank.

Lord Varnwell was instantly contrite. "Forgive me. I just assumed that you were seeking a new mistress. You have given Pandora her congé, have you not?"

His anger became resignation. Bloody hell. It did not seem to matter how diligently he avoided society, it appeared that his movements were still open to speculation. Of course, he inwardly acknowledged, he had known when he had decided to put an end to his lengthy involvement with the elegantly beautiful widow there was bound to be some gossip. The aloof Spanish beauty was one of the most sought-after women in London. The fact that he had willingly ended their liaison was certain to raise brows.

In truth, Anthony had simply grown bored. Although Pandora's cool composure and dislike of excessive emotions had suited his desire for an undemanding companion, he had discovered their occasional interludes becoming increasingly tedious. Ice was all very well and good, but he suddenly realized that he longed for a taste of fire.

Perhaps the fire that shimmered about Miss Cresswell.

"You possess an inordinate interest in my private affairs, Varnwell," he said in soft tones.

"It is entirely your fault," his cousin complained. "If you were not so devilishly secretive about your affairs then the rest of us would not be consumed with curiosity."

"You would prefer that I b—boast of my conquests with all and sundry at the club?"

"It is the accepted practice of most gentlemen."

Anthony's lips twisted. "I rarely bother myself with what is the accepted practice."

"True enough," Varnwell readily agreed. "Still, Miss Cresswell would be a tasty morsel. If you are not interested then I shall continue my pursuit."

The dark eyes narrowed. "You believe her to be open to a liaison?"

"Why else make such a push into society? She can not hope for a respectable offer."

"Why not?"

"Gads, she is the daughter of the Devilish Dandy, the most notorious criminal in England."

"So are her sisters and they have both managed to contract eligible proposals."

Realization dawned with painful slowness. "I say, you are right. Did not one land the Flawless Earl?"

"And the other Lord Hartshore."

"Damn. You believe her to be dangling for a proposal?"

"I haven't the least notion."

Varnwell heaved a deep sigh. "I knew she was too good to be true."

Anthony's gaze shifted to the door through which Miss Cresswell had so recently disappeared.

Was she too good to be true?

Beautiful, passionate, intelligent, and yet utterly innocent beneath her pretense of sophistication?

It was something that he was determined to discover.

TWO

Rachel stifled a yawn as the carriage rattled over the narrow road. She disliked traveling. After several hours on the road her elegant carriage gown was wrinkled and her toes nearly frozen. Even worse she was thoroughly and utterly bored. Only the knowledge that she would soon have her plans of revenge set in motion prevented her from commanding the coachman to return her immediately to the comfort of London.

With an effort she attempted to soothe herself with thoughts of watching the shock and horror upon Lady Broswell's countenance when she discovered that Rachel was to be her close neighbor for the next few weeks.

Along with the Devilish Dandy.

A faint smile curved her chilled lips. In truth she had never intended to accept the invitation to Miss Carlfield's upcoming engagement ball. Although she was very fond of dear Violet, she possessed an abiding dislike for country house parties where one was forced to endure the same guests for days on end. Not to mention the tedious country assemblies, musicales, and teas that were unavoidable. But the knowledge that Broswell Park was less than a mile from Mr. Carlfield's home had swiftly changed her mind. She was about to prove to Lady Broswell that she was far more welcome among Surrey society than she and her pasty-faced daughters.

Across the carriage a tall, leanly muscular gentleman, with gray-streaked dark hair pulled into a tail at his neck, stirred. Attired in an elegant blue coat and silver waistcoat, Solomon Cresswell appeared far too subdued for the Devilish Dandy. Only the brilliant green eyes sparkled with the familiar wicked amusement.

Rachel had not requested that her father accompany her to Surrey. She disliked the notion of him exposing himself in such a manner.

Granted, for years he had kept his criminal activities a secret. Although everyone throughout England and Europe had heard of the dashing and rather romantic Devilish Dandy, his identity was unknown.

Unfortunately that had all changed when a common thug had fingered Solomon as the notorious thief. Without warning, her father had been hauled to Newgate to await the hangman's noose. It had been no less than a miracle that her father had managed to escape unscathed.

Thankfully, the authorities had kept her father well secluded from the curious crowds that had surrounded the prison, hoping for a glimpse of the scandalous thief. Less than a handful had actually caught a glimpse of the Devilish Dandy.

Still, the mere fact that all of England knew that Solomon Cresswell was the Devilish Dandy deepened Rachel's fear he would be recognized. And being in her company would only increase the chance that someone might realize the obvious.

But her father had been adamant. Young ladies did not travel about the countryside on their own, he insisted. And she did not doubt he inwardly worried just how far she might take her desire for revenge.

"Well, my dearest," her father drawled, "we have almost reached our destination. Are you certain you wish to continue onward?"

Rachel lifted her chin in determination. "Of course. I have tolerated enough of Lady Broswell's insults and attempts to shame me out of society."

"You do realize, Rachel, that Lady Broswell is merely attempting to punish me for possessing the audacity to fall in love with her sister? She will never forgive me for sweeping Rosalind away from that debauched marquis that they had chosen for her. As the beauty in the family Rosalind was expected to barter herself for the sake of the family. Which was no doubt why they put out that Rosalind had died rather than admit she had married a gentleman quite beneath her."

Rachel's lips tightened. She did not like being reminded that she was in any way related to Lady Broswell. It was the fact they had driven her father out of the country that had forced him to become a thief to support his wife and growing family. And after all these years only her mother's brother, Lord Scott, revealed the least amount of remorse.

"So you agree that she needs to be punished?" Rachel demanded.

The Devilish Dandy shrugged. "I have always believed that her jealous and bitter nature punishment enough."

"Not on this occasion."

Solomon chuckled. "Ah, my little firebrand. Always so passionate and impulsive. Too much like your father."

"I take that as a compliment."

"So what do you intend to do?"

"Nothing outrageous, I assure you."

Her father's smile was dry. "I wish I could be so easily comforted. You are always outrageous."

"I have been informed that it is a part of my charm," Rachel teased.

"So it is. Along with that very tender heart of yours."

Rachel gave a self-conscious grimace. "What of yourself?"

"What do you mean?"

"What if you are recognized?" she demanded, her hazel eyes dark with concern.

"How could I be?" Solomon smiled with serene confidence in his own abilities. "It is well known that the Devilish Dandy fled to India. Besides, they shall all be too dazzled at encountering Mr. Foxworth, the newest arbitrator of fashion to the Prince."

Rachel gave a shake of her head. She was the only one in England to know of her father's latest charade as the aloof, caustic-tongued gentleman who had captured the Prince's interest. Not even her sisters, Sarah and Emma, realized he was not obeying their command to remain unobtrusive and hidden from proper society.

"You know that Sarah will have your head on a platter if she discovers you are in Surrey? You promised her that you would not deliberately court danger."

"I said that the Devilish Dandy would not court danger," Solomon corrected with a wicked smile. "I said nothing of Mr. Foxworth."

"A fine distinction, especially when Lady Broswell is certain to recognize you. How can you be certain that she will not reveal the truth?"

The lean, handsome features hardened. "She is well aware that I would not hesitate to reveal her very close relationship to the Devilish Dandy. Having managed to insult a great number of the ton over the years she can not afford to risk giving them a reason to slight her."

"I do hope you are right."

"Fear not." Solomon abruptly grimaced as the carriage came to a halt. "Ah, I believe we have arrived. You do realize this promises to be a tedious affair? Whenever engagements are announced the conversation invariably turns to marriage."

Rachel peered out the window to regard the plain stone manor house that had clearly seen better days.

"You are welcome to return to London if you prefer," she said in light tones.

"And leave you here alone? Ah no, my sweet. One Cresswell on the run from the authorities is quite enough."

"Fah." Rachel gathered her muff and reticule. "I intend nothing more than a bit of harmless fun."

"That is what concerns me."

Rachel ignored her father's dry words as the groom opened the door and helped her to alight from the carriage. With determined steps she headed up the stairs, only to come to a halt as the door was pulled open and a plump young maiden with dark curls and childlike beauty rushed out to greet her.

"Rachel," she cried, grabbing Rachel's hand with her own. "I am so very pleased that you came."

A fond smile curved Rachel's lips. She had taken an instant liking to the sweet, rather shy Miss Carlfield since she had made her debut two years before. She had also felt a measure of protectiveness toward the young maiden, who had endured her share of spiteful amusement at her timid nature.

"Violet." She sent her friend a stern frown. "How dare you presume to become engaged without consulting me? You know quite well I have not been allowed to give you my approval."

A surprisingly stricken expression marred the pretty features. "It was all very sudden."

A whisper of unease entered Rachel's heart. "It must have been very sudden. You said nothing of this mysterious suitor in any of your letters to me. Do not tell me that this is a whirlwind courtship?"

"Egads, Rachel, do not quiz the poor child on her doorstep," the Devilish Dandy abruptly chided from behind her shoulder.

Startled, Rachel turned to discover her father regarding Miss Carlfield with a most peculiar expression upon his lean countenance.

Returning her attention to her friend, she offered her a rueful smile.

"Forgive me, Violet. May I introduce my uncle, Mr. Foxworth?"

Violet dropped a proper curtsy. "Mr. Foxworth."

"Enchanted." With a flare most gentlemen could only envy, Solomon claimed the young maiden's hand and lifted it to his lips.

A predictable blush flooded Violet's cheeks as she gazed in the green eyes with a bemused expression.

"Oh."

Rachel's lips twitched. "I fear my uncle insisted that he accompany me."

"A young maiden can not be too careful," her father readily retorted, his gaze never leaving that of Miss Carlfield. "There are many unscrupulous gentlemen who would be quite willing to take advantage of a young, beautiful woman."

Violet's brown eyes darkened in a tragic fashion. "Yes."

"Violet, what do you mean keeping our guests

standing in the cold?" a rough male voice abruptly intruded.

"Father." Miss Carlfield sharply stepped back as a heavy-set gentleman with a florid countenance appeared in the doorway. "May I introduce Miss Cresswell?"

The Honorable Mr. Carlfield gave a cold nod of his head, clearly less pleased at Rachel's presence than his daughter.

"Mr. Carlfield." Rachel's own tone was cold. She had always disliked this gentleman's habit of bullying his only child.

"And her uncle, Mr. Foxworth." Violet finished the introductions.

"Foxworth?" Mr. Carlfield's eyes slowly widened in astonishment. "Not the Fox?"

Swiftly into character, Solomon raised his quizzing glass to stab the man with an icy displeasure.

"Only the Prince has received my permission to refer to me in such an intimate fashion."

Thoroughly enchanted by the notion that his gathering was to be graced by the Prince's current favorite, Mr. Carlfield gave a violent nod of his head.

"Yes, yes. Of course. Such an honor."

"Indeed." Solomon held out his arm for Rachel. "Shall we, my dear?"

"Yes."

They swept through the door as Mr. Carlfield anxiously called for his butler.

"Fallow. Damn your lazy hide where are you? Oh. Fallow, instruct Mrs. Fields to prepare the gold room for Mr. Foxworth."

"The gold room?" the elderly servant demanded in surprise.

"You heard me."

"Yes, sir."

Rachel hid a smile as the butler hurried away. She wondered what poor guest was being evacuated to make room for her father.

Hurrying to take his place at Solomon's side, Mr. Carlfield offered him a tentative smile.

"Perhaps you would care to join me in my library, Mr. Foxworth? I believe I have recently acquired a brandy you will find to your taste."

"Highly unlikely," the Devilish Dandy drawled. "My taste is extraordinarily selective."

"Oh, yes." Mr. Carlfield desperately searched for another means to impress his unexpected guest. "Maybe you would prefer a nice cognac?"

Solomon heaved a sigh. "If you insist. Rachel, I shall see you later."

Of course," Rachel murmured, hiding a smile.

With a royal air, the Devilish Dandy allowed himself to be led toward the library while Rachel turned back to regard her friend, who had lagged behind.

"Now, Violet, I wish to know why you told me nothing of your engagement while you were in London. I can not credit you would keep such a secret from your dearest friend."

Surprisingly the maiden flashed a frightened glance toward her retreating father.

"Perhaps we should speak later."

Rachel was taken aback by her abrupt manner. In her experience young maidens who had just become engaged were vastly enchanted with the notion of droning for hours on the wonder and brilliance of their beloved.

"If you wish."

"I will ensure your rooms are prepared. Excuse me."

With a frown Rachel watched Violet hurry toward the stairs. It was obvious all was not right with the sudden engagement. She briefly considered following after her friend and demanding the truth. Then she gave a shake of her head. No. She would have to wait until Violet was ready to confess her troubles. Only then could she determine how best to help her.

Aimlessly crossing the foyer, Rachel entered the front drawing room, noting the vague air of neglect about the worn carpets and faded curtains. It was becoming obvious that Mr. Carlfield was not as financially sound as he had boasted of in London.

Wondering if this was the reason for Violet's abrupt engagement, Rachel was suddenly startled by the sound of a dark, smoky voice that had haunted her for the past five days.

"Welcome, Miss Cresswell."

Spinning about, she regarded the elegant form of Anthony Clarke with wide eyes.

As he had been during their previous encounter, he was attired almost entirely in black with a striped black-and-white waistcoat. And as on that last occasion the smoldering midnight gaze sent a sharp tingle through her spine and down to the very tips of her toes.

"Mr. Clarke," she breathed in pleasurable surprise. "I did not expect to find you here."

A faint smile curved his lips as he crossed toward her. "I do on occasion receive invitations."

Her hazel eyes sparkled with amusement. Although she had sternly attempted to convince herself that it was merely her imagination that had instilled a shroud of mysterious bewitchment about their brief encounter, she could already feel a heady excitement stirring in the pit of her stomach.

"That is not what I meant. I thought that you preferred your inventions to society."

"S—so I do," he murmured, halting so closely that

she could smell the clean scent of his soap. "It takes a rare temptation to lure me from my workroom."

Her heart tripped as she breathed deeply of his clean, slightly spicy scent. "And what rare temptation brought you to Surrey?"

"I have always enjoyed the country."

Realizing he was teasing her, she gave a click of her tongue. "I do not believe you."

"No? Well, Violet is my cousin. It would have been the height of ill manners to miss her engagement ball."

"I still do not believe you."

The black eyes shimmered with amusement. "P— perhaps I was intrigued by the guest list."

"Any guest in particular?" she demanded with a tiny shiver of excitement.

Anthony smiled, but with the unpredictability that she was beginning to expect of him he abruptly turned the conversation.

"What brings you here, Miss Cresswell? Or am I allowed to guess?"

"If you wish."

"You d—did not choose to heed my words of caution. You seek revenge."

Her chin jutted, the hazel eyes flashing. "Some would call it justice."

"Ah, Miss Cresswell." He chuckled, his hand suddenly raising to trace the line of her neck. "Why would you wish to waste such passion on revenge when there are so many other pleasurable uses for it?"

Her breath caught at the sensation of his slender fingers against her bare skin.

"Mr. Clarke, are you flirting with me?" she asked softly.

"Certainly not. I never flirt."

"Never?"

"Never."

"How very dull."

"Well, I am a rather dull fellow," he retorted, his fingers lingering on the racing pulse at the base of her throat.

Rachel felt mesmerized as she met the midnight gaze. "I think you are fascinating."

His lips twitched. "And I think you are a minx."

"Is that bad?"

"It all depends."

"Upon what?"

"If it is truly your nature or only a means of a disguise."

Rachel frowned. "Disguise?"

"I think, Miss Cresswell, that you enjoy shocking society and dazzling poor susceptible gentlemen until they are too blinded to notice the true woman beneath your sophistication."

Rachel stepped away from his distracting touch. She was suddenly aware that this gentleman was far more dangerous than her usual flirts. Those damnable eyes saw far too much for comfort.

"And I think, sir, that you enjoy speaking in riddles," she retorted in determinedly light tones.

A hint of satisfaction curved his lips as he studied her wary gaze.

"Who was that gentleman I saw you arrive with?"

Rachel paused, not at all certain she liked the manner he could prick through her composure.

"My uncle, Mr. Foxworth."

"H—he looks familiar."

"He should. He is the Prince's current advisor, you know."

A black brow arched. "Is he?"

"You do not sound particularly impressed."

"Probably because I am not."

She gave a reluctant laugh. Anthony Clarke may be the most dangerous gentleman she had ever encountered, but she could not resist the temptation to claim him as another trophy. The very fact he was bound to be far more wily than most gentlemen only added spice to the chase.

"Of course, the elusive Mr. Clarke," she challenged. "Indifferent to the trappings of society."

"You look a great deal like him."

"Oh yes, I very much take after the old Fox."

"Then I shall no doubt find him irresistible," he murmured. "Now, if you will excuse me, I have brought with me a project that I wish to attend to."

Rachel widened her eyes in surprise. "You are leaving me for a project?"

His lips twitched at her disbelieving tone. "Do not fear. There are several other gentlemen about who are no doubt anxious to be dazzled by the charming Miss Cresswell."

"No doubt," she retorted with a hint of annoyance. In her experience gentlemen did not abandon her with such seeming indifference. Could it be that he had not followed her to Surrey? That his presence was nothing more than a coincidence? With a narrowed gaze she watched as he strolled toward the door with languid grace. "Mr. Clarke."

Slowly halting, he turned to face her with a quizzical expression. "Yes?"

"May I be allowed to view your project sometime?"

"I fear it would not hold much interest for you, my dear."

She offered her most enticing pout. "I am interested in many things."

"I shall keep that in mind," he murmured, then with a bow he turned and disappeared from the room.

On her own, Rachel was torn between annoyance and amusement. Anthony Clarke appeared determined to play their little game by his rules. It would be interesting to see who came out the victor.

With a faint shake of her head Rachel moved across the room and into the hall.

She could not allow herself to be distracted by Anthony Clarke. A lighthearted flirtation was all well and good, but she had come to Surrey with a purpose. She very much feared that it would be easy to lose sight of that purpose in a pair of midnight eyes.

Searching for a servant to lead her to her room, Rachel was startled as Violet suddenly raced down the stairs, a handkerchief pressed to her mouth. At the same moment the Devilish Dandy stepped out of the library and moved forward.

The collision was inevitable and Rachel watched from a distance as her father wrapped his arm about the young maiden to keep her upright.

"Forgive me," Violet exclaimed, making no visible effort to free herself from the clutches of the Devilish Dandy.

"There is nothing to forgive," Solomon assured the young lady. "Are you hurt?"

"No."

"Are you certain?" Rachel watched her father lift a hand to touch Violet's cheek. "You have been crying."

"No, there was merely something in my eye."

"It must have been something quite terrible to cause such tears." Solomon reached into his pocket to retrieve a dry handkerchief and pressed it into her hand. "Here."

"You are very kind."

"No, I am rarely kind," the Devilish Dandy admitted wryly. "But I do not wish to see a young maiden in such distress. Perhaps on the next occasion you are troubled with your eyes you will come to me? I can be quite clever in sorting out such difficult situations."

Rachel bit her lip, wondering what the Devil was up to. Violet was clearly troubled and highly vulnerable at the moment. Surely her father would not be so callous as to use her weakness for his own pleasure?

"I fear no one can help me," Violet denied in broken tones. "Excuse me."

Pulling herself free, Violet rushed down the hall. Solomon watched her retreat, unaware of Rachel's approach until she was standing at his side.

"Well, well, Fox. Are you not rather old for such nonsense?" she drawled, only partially teasing.

Surprisingly, the lean features tightened into a rueful grimace.

"Yes. Far too old."

Three

Despite the morning sunshine there was a distinct chill in the air. Pulling his caped greatcoat closer to his body, Anthony leaned negligently against the small grotto at the end of the garden.

It was not the neglected flower beds or fountains that had clearly not functioned in several years that had drawn him from the house. It was not even the lure of following the other gentlemen through the heavy brush in a futile attempt to bag a bird or two.

Oh no, he was on the hunt for something far more delectable than pheasants or grouse, he acknowledged with a flare of anticipation. He was hunting a golden-haired, hazel-eyed minx.

A smile touched his lips. On his arrival in Surrey he had briefly wondered what odd impulse had led him from the pleasures of London. Although Thomas Carlfield was his mother's eldest brother, he had never particularly cared to spend more time than necessary in his company. He found him to be shallow and pompous with careless disregard for his responsibilities. But just a few moments in the company of Miss Cresswell had reminded him of precisely why he had behaved in such an uncharacteristic fashion.

His smile widened. He had been very careful not to overplay his hand. Throughout the previous evening he had taken care to avoid Miss Cresswell. He had been well aware that her hazel gaze had followed him about, calculating and darkened with a hint of annoyance. She expected him to flock about her like the other enthralled gentlemen. To lure her with sweet compliments. It scraped at her pride to think he might be indifferent to her charms.

He did not doubt that she had devoted a great deal of time brooding on how best to bring him properly to heel.

It would be vastly amusing to see how she decided to best accomplish her role.

He did not have long to wait as the sound of approaching footsteps disrupted the silence. Hidden by the grotto, he watched Miss Cresswell wind her way through the twisted paths.

Attired in a brilliant yellow morning gown with a green spencer, she looked unlike any other debutant. There was no pale pastel or simpering manner. Everything about her was vibrantly alive, from her bold choice in fashion to her confident stride. He only wished that her glorious golden curls were not hidden beneath the green bonnet. He would like to see the satin strands flowing about her shoulders.

Waiting until she was nearly upon him, Anthony straightened and stepped onto the path.

"Good morning, Miss Cresswell."

She halted in surprise before a wry smile curved her lips. "Mr. Clarke, you possess an astonishing habit of appearing at the most unexpected places."

"Not unexpected," he denied in soft tones. "Merely logical, my d—dearest."

"Logical?"

He ran a hand down the length of his jaw. "I asked myself this morning what a young lady bent upon revenge would do first. The obvious answer was to seek out her quarry so her game could begin."

She jerked as if startled by his perception, but to her credit her smile never faltered.

"Perhaps I merely wished a short stroll on such a lovely morning."

"If that is the case then you will not mind if I join you."

She regarded him in silence for a long moment, as if determining whether or not he would prove to be a hindrance to her plans before giving a faint shrug.

"If you wish."

Stepping forward, Anthony placed her hand upon his arm and slowly began strolling across the open parkland.

"I suppose I need not tell you that you look lovely this fine morning?"

As if his compliment had suddenly reminded her that she was determined to bewitch him, her expression became coy.

"I must admit I possessed a few qualms about this particular shade of yellow. It appeared rather insipid."

"I defy anything to appear insipid on you."

"How very charming." She allowed her gaze to slowly survey his own form. A sharp, pleasurable heat raced through him. "Do you always wear black, Mr. Clarke?"

"I h—have little interest in the latest fashions. To my mind it is all a great deal of nonsense."

"Do you think so?"

"But of course. Just consider those ridiculous dandies devoting their mornings to preening before a mirror in the hopes of catching your attention, while I have managed to capture you all to myself."

She gave a low chuckle. "Very logical."

"P—precisely."

"But I believe that you have a fault in your logic."

Anthony lifted a dark brow. "And pray what would that be?"

"I do not believe gentlemen devote hours to their appearance in an effort to capture my attention or that of any other lady."

"No?"

"No. I believe it is just another means of attempting to better one another. Like strutting peacocks."

Anthony felt a flare of satisfaction at her shrewd words. He had sensed there was a swift intelligence behind those pretty features. Obviously he had not been mistaken."

"For all your frivolous manner you are very perceptive, my dear."

"Does that surprise you?"

"Not at all." He locked her gaze with his own. "As I have said, I believe that you like to disguise your true self."

She abruptly turned her head, clearly uneasy at the thought that she had revealed more than she had intended. Anthony studied her delicate profile as they crossed a small bridge and entered the fringe of trees that marked the end of Carlfield property. Miss Cresswell was clearly determined to keep a part of herself hidden from the world. He could only wonder what she feared to expose.

He chose a narrow path that forced her to walk closely at his side. The scent of her warm, rose-perfumed skin wrapped about him and he resisted the urge to bring her to a halt and pull her into his arms. It was no doubt precisely what she expected from any gentleman who had managed to lure her into a secluded spot. But he was quite determined to keep her off guard. Miss Cresswell would not be allowed to make him a slave of his own desires. He would be the one in control of their enticing flirtation.

A pity, he inwardly sighed. He was eager to explore that smoldering passion which shimmered about her like a cloak of temptation. Far, far more eager than he had anticipated.

A flame licked through his body. It was a fortunate thing that life had taught him the worth of self-control. He had an uneasy premonition that Miss Cresswell was bound to test his vaunted composure to the very limit.

"What was that?" Miss Cresswell broke into his thoughts.

"What?"

"I saw a flash of something over there."

Without warning the impulsive maiden abandoned his side and plunged through the underbrush without regard to her elegant dress. Momentarily caught off guard, Anthony watched her disappearing through the trees, then with a sudden chuckle he was in swift pursuit.

At least one was never bored when in the company of Miss Cresswell.

Wincing at the scrape of dead branches against the gloss of his Hessians, he swiftly closed the distance, coming up beside her as she halted next to an iron gate set in a stone fence. He glanced about, noting the air of neglect that was settled about the remote property.

"Miss Cresswell, you are not attempting to lure me to a secluded location so that you can t—take advantage of me, are you?" he softly teased.

"Certainly not," she denied pertly.

He heaved a mournful sigh. "A pity."

Reaching out, she pushed at the gate, giving an impatient click of her tongue to find it locked.

"Drat."

"It appears that visitors are not welcome," he murmured, a frown marring his brow as Miss Cresswell promptly reached through the bars to push at the heavy latch. "What the devil are you doing?"

"I want to discover what is being hidden."

He was momentarily taken aback by her strange audacity, then realization struck. "This property belongs to the Broswells', does it not?"

"Precisely." She flashed him a knowing glance.

"You do realize it is highly improper to trespass in such a fashion?" he said dryly.

"Of course." She gave a shrug. "You needn't come with me. I am accustomed to doing the scandalous, but I would not wish to stain your very proper reputation."

He stepped closer, trapping her between the gate and his much larger form.

"Are you attempting to insult me, Miss Cresswell?"

She flashed him an impish grin. "Forgive me. I truly have no desire to embroil you in my evil deeds."

"No one is allowed to embroil me in anything I do not wish to be embroiled in, Miss Cresswell."

"That sounds remarkably like a challenge, Mr. Clarke."

He shrugged. "It is simply the truth."

The long black lashes fluttered in a provocative fashion. "You know, I do not believe I have ever encountered another gentleman precisely like you."

"W—why do you say that?"

"Many reasons." With a bold motion she reached up to pluck a small twig from his coat. "One of which is the fact that you have never once attempted to kiss me."

A heady flare of desire rushed through him. Gads, but he could press her against the gate and take her then and there, if he had been allowed to. She surely had bewitched him. A gentleman could easily be forgiven for losing all sense when faced with such temptation.

"Did you wish me to kiss you, my dear?" he murmured.

"It is a rather predictable occupation of gentlemen."

"I should never wish to be considered predictable."

A hint of frustration darkened her eyes before she abruptly turned back to the gate.

"Then shall we go?"

"By all means." Anthony smiled at her peevish reaction to his elusive game. She was unaccustomed to having her blatant invitations turned aside. With a deliberate motion he moved until he was nearly pressed against her, reaching through the bars to grasp the inner latch. At the same moment he angled his head downward, trailing his lips over the fragrant scent of her bare nape.

"Oh," Miss Cresswell gasped, a sudden shiver shaking her body. "Mr. Clarke."

"Yes, Miss Cresswell?" he whispered as he continued to explore the tantalizing curve of her neck.

"What are you doing?"

The faint quiver in her voice only further inflamed his smoldering desire. He wanted this woman to want him. Not as a conquest or a sop to her female pride. But as a woman in full thrall of her own passions.

"I am attempting to discover if your skin is as satin-soft as it appears."

Her hands grasped the bars as if her knees were threatening to give sway.

"And is it?"

"Oh yes. And it has the most delicious aroma of roses." His arms ached to wrap about her and tug her close to the hardness of his frame. Instead he forced himself to give a sharp pull on the iron latch. "There."

"What?"

"The gate is now open."

"Yes."

With a satisfying lack of grace she stumbled through the opening, clearly anxious to put some distance between them. Anthony followed behind at a more leisurely pace, content for the moment with the knowledge that he had managed to ruffle her practiced air of sophistication. Beneath all that flirtatious manner was an unmistakable innocence, he acknowledged with a smile. Her passions were as untested as those of a schoolgirl.

They moved down an overgrown path, until Miss Cresswell abruptly pointed toward an ivy-covered structure.

"Over there. It looks to be a house."

Anthony briefly studied the square unadorned building. "At a glance I would guess it to be an old dowager house."

"Surely it is empty?"

Anthony cast a glance upward. "There is smoke coming from the chimney."

He intended to convince her that they had intruded far enough. After all, whoever was within the house had gone to considerable lengths to keep out visitors. But with the impulsiveness he was beginning to rue, she was determinedly moving forward.

She rang the bell, then when there was no reply

she overcame the barrier to her goal by the swift process of shoving the door open.

Anthony watched in disbelief as Miss Cresswell calmly moved into the cramped foyer and down the dark hall.

"Hello," she called in bright tones.

With a shake of his head Anthony followed behind, thoroughly expecting to discover a furious farmer armed with a gun.

"Miss Cresswell, you do realize that you are trespassing in a private home?"

"Yes." She came to a halt. "I heard something." With that disconcerting swiftness she was charging down the hall and through an open doorway. Anthony heard her voice float through the air as he was once again in pursuit. "Oh, hello there."

Relieved there was no immediate echo of a gunshot, Anthony entered the room, startled to a halt at the sight of the young maiden settled beside the window in a bath chair.

His narrowed gaze swept over the pale features and too-frail frame. Her blond hair was pulled into a stern bun that only emphasized her hollow cheeks, and her faded gown was clearly too large for her thin body. But there was a clear, restless intelligence in the blue eyes.

"Who are you?" the girl, whom Anthony guessed to be sixteen or seventeen, demanded.

"I am Miss Cresswell and this is Mr. Clarke. Who are you?"

The girl briefly glanced toward the doorway, as if expecting someone to suddenly materialize.

"You should not be here."

Undaunted, Miss Cresswell smiled in a friendly fashion. "We were passing by and I saw something flashing through the trees. I wanted to ensure there was nothing amiss."

"Nothing is amiss."

Anthony stepped closer, noting the object she was attempting to hide in the folds of her skirt.

"Perhaps it was the sun reflecting off your telescope?"

The girl bit her lip. "You should not be here."

"Will you at least tell us your name?" Miss Cresswell asked in gentle tones.

There was a faint pause before the girl turned the wheeled chair better to see them.

"Are you staying at Broswell Park?"

"No, we are guests of Mr. Carlfield," Miss Cresswell explained. "His daughter is becoming engaged to Mr. Wingrove at the end of the month."

Without warning the girl's delicate features hardened. "I don't like him."

Intrigued by the curious maiden living in this seemingly abandoned home, Anthony squatted down to meet her gaze squarely.

"Do you know Mr. Wingrove?"

"No, but he hits his dog with a whip. I don't think a kind man would do that, do you?"

"I certainly do not," Anthony agreed, inwardly deciding to do a bit of investigating in regards to Mr. Wingrove.

The thin face abruptly cleared. "Miss Carlfield looks nice though. She sings when she walks."

Anthony felt a twinge in his heart. Obviously the girl's only connection to the world was through her telescope. He knew better than anyone the heavy loneliness of being secluded from the world.

"She is very, very nice," he agreed with a coaxing smile. "Are you here alone?"

The girl abruptly grimaced. "No, Mrs. Greene is

upstairs sleeping. She always sleeps in the afternoon, which is very lucky for me."

"Is it?"

"Yes." She gave shy smile. "When she goes upstairs I can open the curtains. And sometimes I even go outside, although I am not supposed to."

"Never?" Miss Cresswell exclaimed in shock, her gaze skimming across the dark, barren room.

"Oh no. It is bad for my lungs."

Anthony's brows furrowed. The mere notion of this poor creature being locked in this horrid room day after day made him furious. He did not believe for a moment her lungs were in any danger. She was being hidden away and he fully intended to discover why.

"You have still not told us y—your name," he reminded her.

The blue eyes narrowed with sudden curiosity. "Why do you speak like that?"

Anthony smiled wryly. He was accustomed to those who studiously pretended to ignore his stutter even as they winced in discomfort. Or those who mocked it as a symbol of stupidity. Only Miss Cresswell and this child had reacted with open interest.

He discovered that he far preferred their simple honesty.

"My mother told me that I was kissed by an angel when I was a baby."

The ridiculous tale his mother would tell to comfort her son after he had been ruthlessly teased by the children in the neighborhood seemed to please the girl.

"That must have been very nice."

"Not always." He regarded her in a knowing manner. "Being different from others can be a lonely business."

The blue eyes suddenly darkened an he was allowed to glimpse her deep sadness.

"Yes." They regarded one another in silent understanding, then a faint noise from above had her gripping the arms of her bath chair. "Oh, that is Mrs. Greene. You must go. She will be terribly angry if she finds you here."

"Why?" he demanded.

"Because no one is supposed to be here." She glanced anxiously toward the door. "Please go."

Anthony's opinion of Mrs. Greene was sinking lower by the moment. Not only did she keep the girl trapped like a prisoner in this crumbling, isolated house, but she obviously bullied her as well.

Still, as much as he longed to stay and confront the woman who was clearly charged with the task of caring for the child, he could not do so without having more information about the situation. For the moment the best he could do was avoid causing the girl any trouble.

"Very well," he agreed as he straightened. "It was a pleasure to meet you."

Miss Cresswell flashed him an annoyed glance. "But . . ."

"Come along, Miss Cresswell." He firmly moved to grasp her arm. "We would not wish to create difficulties."

Without giving her an opportunity to protest, he pulled her from the room and down the hall. Even when they were back in the pale sunlight he continued to ruthlessly steer the reluctant woman across the courtyard and back through the gate.

Attempting to free herself, Miss Cresswell glared at his set profile.

"Mr. Clarke, are we in a race?"

"I fear the mysterious Mrs. Green might very well vent her ill temper upon the girl if she discovers our visit."

"Oh."

Miss Cresswell fell silent as they returned to the fringe of trees. Anthony moved them deeper into the shadows before coming to a halt.

"I b—believe we are out of sight."

Wrapping her arms about her waist, Miss Cresswell glanced back toward the distant house.

"That poor child. I dislike leaving her in that house. She is clearly afraid of her nurse. And I do not believe for a moment she is not allowed out because of her lungs. She is being hidden."

Her fierce words were in perfect accordance with his own feelings, but Anthony was not about to admit as much. Not to this madcap, impulsive chit. He would not put it beyond her to charge into the unfortunate situation without considering the consequences to the poor girl.

"Not such an unusual occurrence, I fear," he retorted in steady tones. "Society is very unforgiving of imperfection. There are many families that have chosen to keep a child in seclusion rather than bear the shame of their malady."

Anthony's voice was laced with a bitterness he could not entirely conceal. Although he had managed to dismiss the occasional cruelties and amusement he had encountered over the years, he had never fully managed to heal the wounds inflicted by his own father. Charles Clarke was a cold, distant man with more pride than affection. He had never managed to forgive Anthony for being flawed. It was only his mother's determination that had prevented Charles from abandoning his son to the care of distant relatives.

Miss Cresswell gave a slow shake of her head. "But to lock her in a dark, remote house with no company beyond a surly old woman. It makes me furious to consider a mother who would abandon her own child in such a manner."

"At least she is safe and seemingly well fed. Someone cared enough to at least see to her basic needs."

"Yes," she grudgingly agreed to his logic, then without warning the hazel eyes widened in shock. "Good heavens."

"What?"

"That house." She turned to meet his narrowed gaze. "It must belong to Lady Broswell."

Anthony stiffened, realizing she was more than likely correct in her assumption. The house was on Broswell property. Which meant the girl was somehow connected to the powerful family. A cold chill spread through his body.

"D—do not leap to conclusions, Miss Cresswell," he said, attempting to halt the inevitable.

Predictably she paid him no heed as she allowed the realization to bloom to full fruition.

"How foolish of me not to have noticed the resemblance to the two Miss Hamlin's from the first. The same pale hair, the same blue eyes. If she were properly groomed she could not be mistaken for anything but a sister."

Anthony's expression became grim as he regarded the beautiful countenance.

"And what if she is Lady Broswell's daughter?"

She blinked, as if startled by the sudden steel in his voice. "What?"

"If the child does prove to be the daughter of Lady Broswell, what will you do with such information?"

"I do not comprehend what you are asking."

Anthony drew in a deep breath. He might be fascinated by this lovely minx, but he would not stand aside and watch her use a hapless child in her bid for revenge.

"Then I shall make myself clear." He narrowed his dark eyes. "You came to Surrey with the intention of punishing Lady Broswell for humiliating you at the opera. This morning you managed to stumble across what might be the perfect means of implementing your revenge."

He carefully watched the emotions that rippled over her delicate features. Confusion, disbelief, and at last a blazing fury.

"Mr. Clarke, I may be impetuous and even frivolous, but I am not a monster," she gritted. "I would never, ever do anything to harm that poor child."

A sharp, fierce flare of relief rushed through Anthony. It was quite obvious that the volatile Miss Cresswell was not as calculating as he had briefly feared. Indeed, she appeared deeply offended by the mere suggestion that she would use the girl for her revenge.

"I n—never thought you a monster, my dear," he assured her in gentle tones, "but it would have to be a temptation. To expose such a scandal might very well ruin Lady Broswell."

Miss Cresswell was not appeased by his logic. In fact, Anthony was suddenly very relieved that looks could not kill.

"I have no need to use crippled children to fight my battles, sir."

With a toss of her head she turned to stalk through the trees back toward the Carlfield house.

Left on his own, Anthony allowed a smile to curve his lips.

She was magnificent in her anger.

A wild, impetuous, passionate creature.

The challenge of capturing such a female was irresistible, he acknowledged. He slowly turned to follow in her wake.

The hunt was on.

Four

Although he took care to maintain his role of the ennui-plagued gentleman, Mr. Carlfield could barely contain his glee at having a renowned favorite of the Prince beneath his roof. In an effort to make sure that his neighbors could properly appreciate his good fortune, invitations to dinner were hastily delivered to all the best houses.

Knowing that the Broswell household would be included in the invitations, Rachel dressed with care.

Her gown was a rose satin slip with a white lace overskirt. The hem was set with a deep flounce of lace with dark roses. The bodice was cut low to emphasize her lovely curves and the large ruby pendant lay upon her white skin like a flame of temptation. She pulled back her hair in a simple knot, with a few golden curls left to brush her temples.

When at last satisfied she was appearing her best, Rachel made her way down to the formal salon and situated herself in a prominent position so that she could thoroughly enjoy the expression on Lady Broswell's countenance when she noticed her presence.

She was forced to wait nearly half an hour for the lady to appear, but she was not disappointed when the lofty woman swept into the room and abruptly froze in horror. The pale blue eyes narrowed and the condescending smile slipped from the thin lips. Her horror only deepened at the sight of the tall, lean gentleman attired in a pearl-gray coat and black pantaloons, who was negligently leaning against the mantel. Nearly breathing fire, she stormed across the carpet to openly confront Rachel.

"You." She spat out the word with a healthy dose of venom. "How dare you come to Surrey, you forward jade?"

Rachel allowed a small, contented smile to touch her lips. "Good evening, Lady Broswell. A lovely party, is it not?"

The calm greeting only deepened the fury in the pale eyes. "I asked you why you followed me."

"Follow you?" Rachel gave a tinkling laugh. "Do not be absurd. I am here at the invitation of Miss Carlfield. She is a very dear friend."

Lady Broswell clenched her hands into fists, clearly having forgotten the crowd of glittering guests who were spilling into the room.

"Fah. I do not believe that for a moment."

"You are, of course, welcome to believe what you will."

"You are here to attempt to embarrass me," she accused, her gaze shifting to where the Devilish Dandy sipped his brandy in a bored fashion. "You and that black-hearted scoundrel."

Rachel's expression hardened at the shrill words. This woman was not fit to polish her father's boots. She had turned her back on her own sister, she refused to acknowledge her nieces, she was attempting to bully a hapless gentleman into marriage with her daughter, and worst of all, she was hiding a crippled child in a dark, isolated house with a woman who was indifferent to her happiness. She was a heartless, selfish witch.

"I suggest that you take care in how you refer to my father, Lady Broswell," she warned in icy tones.

Momentarily taken aback, the woman attempted to bluster Rachel into retreat.

"I want you to leave."

"That is unfortunate since I have promised Miss Carlfield to stay for her engagement ball. Besides, Mr. Carlfield has taken a decided liking to my uncle Foxworth."

A dark flush stained the older woman's countenance as she realized she had come to dinner in honor of a man who was in truth Solomon Cresswell.

"I have no doubt his ridiculous fascination with Mr. Foxworth would come to an unpleasant end if he were to discover that he was no more than a common thief."

Rachel did not so much as flinch at the blatant threat. "But he will not discover any such thing."

"You can hardly be certain," the woman hissed.

"Oh yes, I can. Because if there is even the slightest hint that my father is anyone but Mr. Foxworth, then I will see to it that everyone in Surrey is aware of our close family connection, dear aunt."

A sharp, brittle silence fell as Lady Broswell struggled to contain her flaming temper. Rachel did not doubt that she longed to screech at her like a fishwife. It was only the knowledge that she would be the source of amusement among her neighbors that kept her tone lowered.

"You would not dare."

"I will do so with pleasure."

The massive bosom heaved with frustration. "You will be sorry for this."

Rachel gave a slow shake of her head. "No, you

are the one who will be sorry for the manner in which you have treated me."

Abruptly realizing the dangerous glint in Rachel's eyes, Lady Broswell regarded her warily. "What is that supposed to mean?"

Rachel gave a faint shrug. "I have heard the unfortunate rumors that your daughters have once again failed to receive an offer during the Season."

The thin lips nearly disappeared as the thrust slid home. It was no secret that Lady Broswell had been sorely disappointed that neither of her daughters had managed to contract a brilliant match. Or even a respectable match. The fact that both misses were of high birth with large dowries only deepened the humiliation of their utter failure.

Of course, she was not about to reveal her inner humiliation to Rachel. Instead she gave a loud sniff.

"As is only proper, my daughters are excessively particular. They have no interest in gentlemen who would flock about the more vulgar members of society."

She left no doubt that Rachel was among those vulgar members.

"Indeed." Rachel deliberately widened her smile. "Then you are no longer attempting to bring Lord Newell up to scratch?"

The woman stiffened in outrage. "Lord Newell is very devoted to Mary."

"No, he is devoted to his quarterly allowance which he fears will be brought to an end if you complain to his mother. It is well known that you and Lady Newell have attempted to bully him into marriage since he came of age."

"You know nothing of the matter, but how could you?" Lady Broswell grated, the plumes in her gray hair quivering in a ridiculous fashion. "Women of your stamp could have no notion of family duty."

The notion of having this woman lecture family duty to her sent a bolt of fury through Rachel. How dare she? Rachel would never turn her back on her sisters. Or treat a poor child as an unwanted mistake to be tossed aside.

Still, she had promised herself that she would not be goaded into losing sight of her goal. It was imperative that she remain in command of the confrontation.

"Perhaps not, but I do know when a lamb is being led to the slaughter," she said with cool mockery. "You know, I almost pity Mary. It can not be pleasant to realize that her prospective bridegroom would rather have a tooth drawn than wed her."

Clearly indifferent to the thought of condemning her daughter to an empty marriage, Lady Broswell gave her a superior glare.

"Mary accepts her responsibility. Unlike your mother."

The hazel eyes flared with an effort to maintain her temper. "My mother accepted that following her heart was more important than the dismal trappings of a loveless marriage. She enjoyed more happiness in her short life than you will ever know in your entire bitter existence."

A stunned silence followed her sharp words and before Lady Broswell could adequately recover, the tall form of Mr. Clarke appeared at Rachel's side.

A brief flicker of irritation at the interruption raced through Rachel until she lifted her head and met the deep brown eyes. In that moment, even her earlier pique at his accusation that she would use a helpless child to enact her revenge was forgotten. For all his strength and smoldering masculinity there was a tenderness in those eyes that made her heart quiver and her knees weak.

"Miss Cresswell, I believe that Violet is searching for you," he said in his soft tones.

Knowing that she had at least lodged a prick of unease in Lady Broswell, Rachel gave a gracious nod of her head.

"Thank you, Mr. Clarke."

"I will escort you to her."

Seeing Lady Broswell gnash her teeth at the eligible gentleman's interest in her, Rachel readily placed a hand on his proffered arm. With her head held high she allowed herself to be led through the thickening crowd, barely paying heed to the numerous gentlemen attempting to capture her attention.

It was not until she was neatly turned through a doorway that she abruptly glanced about to discover that Mr. Clarke had pulled her into the library and that he was even now firmly closing the door behind him.

"Did Miss Carlfield wish to meet me here?" she asked in surprise.

Smiling, he strolled to tower over her. "No, I merely thought that it was time to intervene. The sparkle in your lovely eyes had grown distinctly dangerous and Lady Broswell's complexion was becoming the shade of an overripe plum."

Rachel shrugged her unconcern at the nasty encounter. "She was rather displeased to discover that I am a guest of Mr. Carlfield."

"That was fairly obvious," he stated in dry tones.

"She very desperately wished to command me to leave. Unfortunately for her I do not accept commands from anyone."

His head suddenly tilted back to emit a low

chuckle. "You have no need to tell me, Miss Cresswell. You are shockingly perverse."

She met his gaze squarely. "Thank you."

"S—so, your games begin."

"Yes." She slowly narrowed her gaze. "And you need not fear that I will use that poor girl in my evil plot."

The dark gaze moved over her delicate features. "I see that I am still not forgiven. My only defense was my concern for the child."

"You seem to have a very low opinion of me, Mr. Clarke."

"On the contrary, Miss Cresswell, my opinion of you increases every passing moment," he returned in low, smoky tones. "You are quite fascinatingly unique."

Rachel sucked in a sharp breath, recalling the feel of his warm lips trailing over the sensitive skin of her neck. Heavens, she had nearly fallen to her knees at the heady pleasure that had flooded through her body. She had never experienced anything so shockingly delightful. Not even the most experienced rogues had managed to create the faintest flutter within her.

The knowledge that this gentleman had managed to arouse her senses with such ease should no doubt have terrified her. It made her vulnerable in a manner she was uncertain how to battle. Instead she shivered with a delicious excitement. A little risk always added pleasure to her day.

"Do you really think so?" she asked in coy tones.

His lips twitched, almost as if he could read her very thoughts. "Yes. And perhaps a bit dangerous."

"Dangerous?"

"Tell me, my dear, are you always so swift to enact justice upon those you feel have wronged you?"

Rachel abruptly lowered her eyes. She realized that to Mr. Clarke her behavior must appear outlandish. He could not know that the revenge she intended to enact was as much for her mother as for herself. That was something she could never confess.

"The night of the opera was not the first occasion Lady Broswell has attempted to shame me from society," she retorted with a lift of her hands. "She has devoted considerable energy to spreading nasty rumors and vicious lies. Do you feel I should simply ignore her insults?"

A slender hand reached out to cup her chin and gently press her face upward to meet his dark, probing gaze. Rachel shivered as the heat of his fingers seared her skin.

"Unfortunately Lady Broswell is not the only sharp-tongued shrew within society. I can not believe that others have not offered you insult."

She stiffened at his words. "Because I am the daughter of the Devilish Dandy?"

The dark gaze swept over her with open admiration. "Because you are a vibrant, beautiful maiden who collects gentlemen with the ease most women collect jewels. It is bound to create jealousy. So why Lady Broswell?"

Rachel suddenly realized that she would have to take care. This gentleman was no witless dandy. He would not be easy to fool.

"She annoyed me."

"You did not travel to Surrey because you were annoyed," he persisted.

With a swift motion she pulled away from his touch, knowing she needed her wits fully about her.

"I have told you the truth."

He studied her for a long, unnerving moment. "There is more to this than you are willing to reveal, but I s—shall not press you. In time you will confide in me."

Much to her surprise Rachel realized that she wished she could confide in this man. There was a strength and steadfastness about him that inspired her instinctive trust. But the secret was not hers alone. She was not in the position to reveal the truth.

"You are very certain of your charms," she teased in an effort to distract him.

She perhaps succeeded too well as a fire smoldered to life in his dark eyes.

"But of course. They are irresistible, you know."

"Are they?"

"Oh yes," he murmured, then with a slow, deliberate motion he lowered his head and pressed his lips to her bare shoulder.

Rachel gasped, feeling as if she had been branded. He did not grasp her or attempt to hold her in any manner. It would have been a simple matter to step from his caress. But she did not move. Indeed, she was quite certain she could not have twitched a muscle.

His lips tasted, stroked, and nibbled her shoulder, sending violent shudders through her body. Her lashes fluttered downward as she became lost in the utter pleasure sizzling through her.

She did not know what it was about this gentleman that set her senses on fire. And at the moment she did not care. She only wanted to close her eyes and drown in her stirring passions.

His lips trailed a blazing path over the delicate line of her collarbone, lingering on the fluttering pulse at the base of her throat. He gave a low growl of satisfaction at her obvious response to his touch.

"I am developing a deep, lingering appreciation for the scent of roses," he muttered against her throat.

Her hands lifted to grasp the lapels of his black jacket. It was that or melt to her knees.

"Mr. Clarke, you should not be doing this."

He chuckled, boldly nipping her skin with the edge of his teeth.

"Do you wish me to halt?"

Rachel was incapable of playing her role as the coy flirt. "No."

"Neither do I." The lips stroked upward and Rachel parted her mouth in anticipation of his long-awaited kiss. But the kiss never arrived and reluctantly lifting her lashes, she discovered he had pulled back to regard her flushed countenance with tense restraint.

"I think it would be best if we return to the others."

Rachel longed to protest. She did not want to bring an end to the sweet passion he had stirred to life. But belatedly realizing that the midst of a large party was hardly the setting for such activities, no matter how entrancing, brought her sharply to her senses.

"Yes."

He smiled gently into her darkened eyes. Before he could speak, however, the door to the library was thrust open and a tall gentleman with gray-streaked hair pulled to the nape of his neck stepped into the room.

Rachel discretely shifted away from Mr. Clarke as she met her father's speculative gaze.

"Rachel," the Devilish Dandy murmured. "I wondered where you had disappeared to."

"We were just returning."

The green gaze briefly shifted toward the silent Mr. Clarke before he moved forward to offer Rachel his arm.

"Perhaps it would be best if I escort you back to

the salon. I should not wish unpleasant speculation to arise from your appearance together."

She hesitated only a moment before placing her hand on his arm. She did not dare glance at Mr. Clarke, knowing that she was certain to reveal precisely what had been occurring before her father's arrival.

In silence the Devilish Dandy led her back into the crowded room, firmly steering her toward a distant corner before coming to a halt and regarding her in a stern manner.

"You appear to be on very friendly terms with Mr. Clarke," he accused in smooth tones.

Rachel could not halt the smile that curved her lips. "He is a unique gentleman."

"Most women in England appear to think so," her father agreed dryly.

She gave an impatient click of her tongue. "I do not mean his fortune. Many gentlemen are wealthy. He is a mystery."

"He is also intelligent, eccentric, and indifferent to the usual rules of society." The green eyes narrowed. "Not at all the sort to be a dutiful sycophant."

"No," she agreed, not nearly so disturbed by the knowledge as she should have been.

A short silence fell before her father smiled in a wry manner. "You will have a care, will you not, my dear?"

"What do you mean?"

"I have learned over the years that there are rare individuals who will not be deceived, manipulated, nor seduced. They can not be controlled, which is always dangerous."

She did not need her father's warning to know that Mr. Clarke was dangerous. She sensed his danger in every glance and every touch.

"I shall keep your warning in mind."

"See that you do, or you might find yourself the one on the leash."

Rachel widened her eyes in outrage. "Never."

"We shall see."

Any protest Rachel might have desired to utter at the absurd warning was halted as their host came bearing down upon them with a thin, dour-faced gentleman with graying brown hair.

"Mr. Foxworth, there you are," Mr. Carlfield cried in a hearty voice. "I wished to introduce you to Mr. Wingrove. Mr. Wingrove, this is Mr. Foxworth, a close acquaintance of the Prince."

Rachel stiffened in shock. This dried-up gentleman was engaged to Violet? Gads, he was old enough to be her father. And there was a sour, unpleasant cast to his hatchet features. Surely her dear friend could not have willingly chosen such a repulsive suitor?

With a prim sniff, Mr. Wingrove regarded the Devilish Dandy with glittering disapproval.

"The Prince?" He sneered. "I fear I possess nothing but disgust for the fop. A most obscene and unsavory character. Nothing at all like his father."

Mr. Carlfield stiffened in dismay at the man's traitorous disregard for England's royal Prince. The Devilish Dandy, however, smiled in a manner that made Rachel feel a pang of sympathy for the stiff-rumped fool. No one bested Solomon Cresswell.

"True. The Prince rarely needs to be locked in his room due to madness, nor does he foam at the mouth when his will is crossed."

"How dare you, sir?" Mr. Wingrove demanded, his eyes bulging like a toad.

The Devilish Dandy shrugged. "Quite easily."

"Our King demonstrates the finest of English sensibilities. He is an upstanding and righteous gentleman. Nothing at all like his wastrel of a son."

Solomon flicked a mocking glance at the gentleman who was quivering with outrage.

"He is a dull, plodding, incompetent fool who managed to lose the greater part of our colonies."

For a moment Rachel thought the rat-faced man might jump up and down in his frustrated anger. Then, clearly anxious to avoid an unpleasant scene, Mr. Carlfield loudly cleared his throat."

"Yes, well, this is a party. Shouldn't argue politics in front of the ladies, you know."

Neither gentleman paid him the least heed as they continued to regard one another in open contempt.

"No doubt Mr. Foxworth prefers to discuss the latest gossip from London or perhaps the current styles in fashion."

Remaining annoyingly aloof, the Devilish Dandy calmly withdrew his snuffbox to carefully measure out a pinch of the scented mix.

"I am certainly a notable expert on fashion."

"Fah. A waste of a true gentleman's intellect."

"You would think so, of course."

Mr. Wingrove pursed his lips as he watched the elegant gentleman replace his snuffbox and carefully wipe his hand on a lace handkerchief.

"And what precisely does that mean?"

"Any gentleman willing to employ a valet with such a painful lack of talent in tying a cravat must be indifferent to good taste. I should have him hung at first light if I were you."

The thin face darkened to an interesting shade of purple. "I have no desire to appear like a ridiculous dandy."

"No doubt a wise choice," Solomon drawled. "A gentleman must possess an elegance of form to carry off true style." Ignoring the man's gasp of fury, he grasped Rachel's elbow. "Come along, my dear. There must be someone of interest among this dreary gathering to converse with."

Rachel smothered her laugh as her father swept her regally away, leaving behind a sputtering Mr. Wingrove.

"That went rather well," she teased as they moved through the crowd.

"Pompous twit," Solomon muttered.

"Yes, indeed."

"What is Mr. Carlfield thinking to tie his daughter to such a grim, ill-humored gentleman?"

Rachel regarded him in surprise. It was unlike her father to concern himself with another's troubles. He far preferred to laugh at the follies of society than to become involved. She could only wonder how Miss Carlfield had managed to stir him to such obvious annoyance.

"I do not believe Mr. Carlfield is interested in his prospective son-in-law's personality. He obviously has more pressing concerns."

The Devilish Dandy's lips thinned as he pointedly glanced about the shabby room.

"Yes. He is selling her to the highest bidder."

"Hardly an unusual occurrence. Few women are as fortunate as myself to have a father who is clever enough to create his own fortune without bartering off his daughters."

She expected her light words to bring a smile to his face. Instead his brows furrowed in an uncharacteristic fashion.

"It should be a crime."

A tingle of unease raced through Rachel as she came to a halt and gazed at her father with a steady regard. She did not understand precisely what had occurred between her father and Miss Carlfield, but she did know that his practiced charms could be lethal to an innocent maiden.

"You offered me a warning moments ago," she said in firm tones. "Now, I shall return the favor."

He raised his brows. "Indeed?"

Most would have crumpled beneath the cool warning in the green eyes. Rachel, however, was very much her father's daughter.

"Miss Carlfield is very frightened and vulnerable at the moment," she retorted bluntly. "She could be easily hurt."

Solomon appeared sincerely startled by Rachel's warning. "I would never hurt her."

"I do hope not." Rachel allowed her gaze to move to the pale, sad maiden currently attempting to sink into the shadows. "I fear she has been hurt enough."

Five

Anthony had debated long over his choice of presents to take to the child in the dowager house. He had any number of trinkets he had built that might prove intriguing to an intelligent girl. Still, he had wanted something that might help occupy her through her long days of boredom. Something that would ease her loneliness.

He had at last hit upon the boxes of wooden puzzles he had brought as gifts for the children in the neighborhood. The puzzles were simple polished walnut that he had hand-carved. They were unpainted, but instead created various shapes when they were put together. To make them difficult enough to occupy her agile mind he had tumbled several puzzles together and put them in a lacquer box with a pretty Chinese garden painted on top.

He had not been disappointed in the girl's reaction to his gift. Seated once again in her bath chair beside the window, her thin face had lit with unabashed pleasure as she had reverently stroked the polished puzzle pieces. He had even managed to coax her to reveal that her name was Julia and that she was sixteen years of age.

He knew that his stammer helped to ease her discomfort with the strange gentleman who had intruded into her solitary world. Like her, he was different from others and that provided a bond they could both sense.

They were busily discussing the best means of keeping the puzzles hidden from Mrs. Greene, who was once again locked in her rooms for the afternoon, when a faint noise had him turning about to discover Miss Cresswell standing in the doorway, holding a large basket.

His breath caught at the lovely vision. Attired in a mulberry gown with a black spencer, she was a vivid beauty in the drab darkness. It was little wonder that he had lain awake half the night plagued with the memory of her warm satin skin beneath his lips, he wryly acknowledged.

Ironically, his deliberate seduction in the library had been designed to ignite the flames of her own untested passions. He knew she had been caught off guard by his first caresses earlier in the day. It had seemed rather clever to press his advantage while she was still vulnerable.

What he had not expected was the fierce, hungry desire that had clutched him the moment he had touched her. Dash it all, he was a grown gentleman, not an overeager schoolboy. He had possessed the most beautiful mistress in all of London. But he had known his mistake the moment he had felt the searing heat flood his lower body. He had not even dared to pull her into his arms for fear he might sweep her off her feet and tumble her onto the nearby couch.

His near lack of control had never occurred before. And neither had the dull ache that had kept him tossing and turning most of the night.

Oddly, however, the realization did not deter his

temptation to pursue her. His fascination was not yet sated and he could not walk away.

With a smile he offered her a faint bow. "Good day, Miss Cresswell."

She regarded him with a clear, steady gaze that was unclouded by maidenly confusion or embarrassment. He discovered that he admired her refusal to pretend a dismay for their shared moment of desire.

"I did not realize you would be here, Mr. Clarke."

"I brought Julia a gift."

"Julia." Miss Cresswell smiled kindly at the young girl in her chair as she moved forward. "What a pretty name."

As dazzled by Miss Cresswell's potent charm as everyone else, the girl regarded her with shy appreciation.

"Thank you."

"What has Mr. Clarke brought for you?"

Julia readily held out her open box to reveal the wooden pieces.

"Puzzles."

"Actually there are ten puzzles," Anthony said. "It will be up to Julia to sort them out and discover which pieces belong to which puzzles."

The blue eyes lit with enthusiasm. "It shall be great fun."

Miss Cresswell abruptly turned to meet his dark gaze. "Did you make these?"

"Yes."

"Are they not lovely?" Julia breathed.

"Quite, quite lovely," Miss Cresswell agreed. "I fear my gift is vexingly paltry in comparison."

Anthony took a deep sniff. "It does, however, smell far more appetizing."

Miss Cresswell smiled. "I thought it would be a lovely afternoon for a picnic."

"A delightful notion."

Julia's eyes widened. "You mean outside?"

"The sun is quite warm," Miss Cresswell swiftly assured the girl.

"I do not believe Mrs. Greene would approve."

"Then we must be very certain that we do not awaken her."

Anthony glanced toward the open bottle of brandy set on a table. "I doubt an invasion by Napoleon could awaken her at the moment."

Following his gaze, Miss Cresswell grimaced. Then, with a determined air, she reached into the basket to reveal a cloak.

"Here, I have brought this to keep you warm," she said, wrapping the garment around the girl's slim shoulders.

"You are certain we will not be caught?"

Miss Cresswell brushed a hand over the pale curls. "Trust me."

There was a pause before Julia gave a nod of her head. "Very well."

At a glance from Miss Cresswell, Anthony willingly moved to scoop Julia into his arms so that he could carry her from the dark house. His heart clenched at the painful frailness of her form. What the girl needed was fresh air and decent food, he thought with a flare of disgust toward her family. And the loving concern of someone who truly cared for her.

With Miss Cresswell leading the way, they moved out of the house and toward a sunny patch of grass well hidden by an unkempt hedge. With swift movements she spread out a blanket, then as Anthony lowered Julia onto the cover, she began to unload the large platters of pheasants, cream potatoes, fresh trout, peas, strawberries, and custard.

He shared a smile with Miss Cresswell as Julia's eyes widened with disbelief as she was handed several plates of the tempting feast. With obvious delight the girl tackled the mounds of food, thankfully unaware she was supposed to pretend a feminine delicacy. Miss Cresswell also revealed a hearty appetite, displaying the same passionate delight for food as she did for everything else in life.

Anthony found their company a refreshing change from most companions at picnics. There were few things more off-putting than females barely nibbling at their food and shrieking at every ant and bee that might happen by.

At last satisfied, Julia leaned back and heaved a happy sigh.

"I have never tasted anything so wonderful. Do you always eat so grandly?"

"This is not so grand as some dinners," Miss Cresswell assured her. "It is said that the Prince will have as many as twenty-five dishes during just one serving and that his dinner can last as long as four hours."

"So much?" Julia breathed in disbelief.

Anthony gave a shake of his head. "T—too much."

"Have you attended a meal with the Prince?" Miss Cresswell demanded.

"As it so happens, I have," Anthony confessed, recalling with a shudder the hours he had spent in Brighton Pavilion upon the Prince's command.

Julia regarded him in awe. "What was it like?"

"Hot, smoky, and so crowded that one could barely breathe," he retorted honestly. "I can readily assure you that this pleasant meal with two beautiful maidens is much more to my liking."

"Very charming, Mr. Clarke," Miss Cresswell said.

He met her sparkling gaze. "Well, there are those who claim that my charm is irresistible."

"Oddly, I have only heard that particular claim made by yourself," she charged.

"Then clearly you have not been conversing with the proper people."

"Indeed?"

Oblivious to the flirtatious banter, Julia smiled in a dreamy fashion.

"I should love to attend such a gathering. All those lovely women in beautiful gowns and gentlemen leading them onto the dance floor."

"I f—fear that they are vastly overrated, my dear," Anthony warned. "The entertainments usually consist of ripping reputations to shreds while the majority of gentlemen with any sense seek the back rooms for a private game of cards."

The delicate features abruptly crumpled in disappointment. "Oh."

Anthony grimaced as Miss Cresswell sent him a chiding frown. "Do not pay any heed to Mr. Clarke, he is merely teasing you."

"Yes, indeed," Anthony quickly agreed. "Please forgive me."

"And someday you will enjoy such parties yourself," Miss Cresswell promised.

"Oh no." Julia shook her head. "That will never be possible."

"Anything is possible, is that not so, Mr. Clarke?"

"Absolutely. You only have to wish hard enough."

The blue eyes searched his countenance. "Do you truly believe so?"

He did not hesitate. "Yes."

"What would you wish for, Julia?" Miss Cresswell demanded.

She smiled in a shy manner. "A new gown in a

lovely shade of blue with lace about the hem. And to attend a ball. And . . ." The girl's words trailed away as a flush stained her cheeks.

"Yes?" Anthony gently prompted.

"You will think me foolish."

"Impossible. What do you wish?"

"To fly like a bird," she confessed shyly. "I told you that it was foolish."

"Not at all. It is a wonderful wish," Miss Cresswell said firmly, then suddenly turned to regard him with a teasing glance. "And what of you, Mr. Clarke? What would you wish for?"

Anthony took a moment to consider his answer. "To view the wonders of China. To touch the stars. To discover a warm, passionate woman to fill my life."

Her breath seemed to catch as her eyes widened. "Sir."

He gave a pleased chuckle at her response. "And now I believe that it is your turn, Miss Cresswell."

Readily recovering, she gave a shrug. "Well, I should wish for a lovely town house in an elegant neighborhood. The pleasure of my sisters' company. And"—she paused before giving a wry smile—"my father free of danger."

Anthony studied her for a long moment, considering her obvious close ties to her family. He experienced a faint flare of envy. Despite their scandalous and highly unconventional life, they possessed a far greater bond than he felt toward his more respectable family.

"You do not wish for a h—husband and family?" he probed with undeniable curiosity.

She gave a startled blink at his unexpected question. "Goodness, no. I am enjoying my independence.

Why would I desire to sacrifice it for any gentleman?"

His gaze narrowed at her deliberate challenge. "There would surely be some benefits?"

"Not nearly enough to tempt me."

He leaned slowly forward. "Perhaps you have not yet tasted true temptation."

Their gazes locked and Anthony was seized with an unbearable urge to close the small distance and capture her lips with his own. Gads, but she had bewitched him. But even as his body tingled in anticipation, an empty plate was suddenly thrust beneath his nose.

"May I have more strawberries?" Julia demanded, unaware of the pulsing shimmers that filled the air between her companions.

With an overly brisk motion Miss Cresswell refilled her plate and then busied herself with wrapping the remaining food into napkins.

"Here. We shall make sure these are properly covered and you may save them for a midnight treat."

The blue eyes lit with pleasure. "Oh."

With reluctance Anthony rose to his feet, knowing they had tempted fate long enough.

"I should return Julia inside. We would not wish to have Mrs. Greene discover our secret."

Miss Cresswell gave a nod of her head. "Yes. I will finish packing our things."

Once again scooping the girl into his arms, Anthony returned her to the bath chair and removed the cloak to replace it with a nearby blanket. He was pleased to note that her cheeks appeared nicely colored from her brief time outside and her eyes sparkled with happiness. She had obviously enjoyed her afternoon.

"Do not forget to keep the food and puzzles hidden beneath the blanket," he warned, knowing that there would be trouble if the items were discovered.

"I will," Julia promised, then regarded him with an uncertain expression. "You will return?"

"Certainly," he promised.

"Thank you for a lovely picnic."

"It is I who should thank you for being such a charming companion." He gallantly raised her thin fingers to his lips. "Good-bye, my dear."

Leaving the room, he carefully listened to make sure that there were no sounds from above before hurrying from the house. He discovered Miss Cresswell waiting for him beside the gate and taking the basket from her, he carefully relatched the lock and led her toward the nearby trees.

"Your picnic was a charming notion," he congratulated his companion, delighted to have her alone for the moment.

"It was too lovely a day to remain inside."

"Still there must have been any number of entertainments offered for your enjoyment this afternoon."

She gave a casual lift of one shoulder. "None that captured my interest."

Anthony gave a low chuckle as he gazed down at the lovely countenance. "Why will you not just admit that you were performing a good d—deed? You need not fear that I will reveal the dazzling Miss Cresswell does indeed possess a heart."

A hint of unease darkened her eyes before she gave a toss of her head.

"You are being absurd." She brushed aside a limb hovering in the path then gave a small exclamation. "What is that?"

"What?"

She bent downward then rose to reveal a delicate piece of jewelry studded with diamonds and pearls.

"It is a brooch."

Anthony regarded the small treasure with a lift of his brows. "A very expensive brooch."

"What would it be doing here?"

He hid a smile, suspecting that she was deliberately attempting to change the subject. She was far more comfortable with her image as a callous flirt than a kindhearted innocent.

"I assume that it must have fallen from some lady's gown."

She flashed him a frown. "Here?"

"You are not the only lady who is capable of walking on a fine day."

Her lips thinned at his light tone. "I find it difficult to imagine Lady Broswell or her daughters strolling through the woods no matter how fine the day, Mr. Clarke. They are far too concerned a bit of dust might mar their hems."

He had to admit that she did have a point. Lady Broswell would not be one to consider nature as anything but a nuisance.

"Then perhaps it belongs to Miss Carlfield," he suggested as they continued through the trees and stepped into the parkland.

"Yes, I shall ask her," Miss Cresswell murmured, seemingly intrigued by her discovery.

In silence they moved toward the house, but as they entered the courtyard Anthony came to a halt.

"I shall part from you here, my dear."

She regarded him in surprise. "You are not going into the house?"

"No, I have a project I wish to begin," he informed her firmly.

As expected, her eyes flashed with annoyance at being so summarily dismissed.

"Yet another project?" she demanded.

"Yes."

She gave a small sniff. "I do hope you never intend to wed, Mr. Clarke. I fear a wife would find your habit of forever disappearing to attend to your projects rather tedious."

He smiled with calm indifference to her barb. "Perhaps I shall choose a woman I feel worthy of being included in my projects."

"No doubt she will feel honored."

"No d—doubt."

For a moment she struggled to pretend an aloof disinterest in his movements. She was not a woman who pursued a gentleman. They were meant to pursue her. But his air of mystery at last got the better of her.

"Can you at least tell me what this secret project is?"

"Of course," he agreed with a shrug. "I am going to make a young girl's wish come true."

It was obviously not what she had expected and she blinked in surprise. "What?"

"Somehow I am going to see to it that Julia is allowed to fly like a bird."

There was a shocked silence, then quite without warning, she had grasped his face between her hands and pressed her lips to his own.

It was their first true kiss and Anthony was swift to respond. Dropping the basket he wrapped his arms about her and tugged her close. He was indifferent to the knowledge that they were standing in the middle of the courtyard. Or that this had not been plotted into his well-calculated seduction. All that mattered was that she was at last in his arms, where she belonged.

Her mouth was sweet honey heat making his head swim and his thighs tighten. He sucked in the scent of roses, tasting deeply of her innocence. With gentle care he urged her lips apart, allowing him access to the tender warmth of her mouth. She gave a soft moan, then with gratifying reluctance, she pulled back to meet his smoldering gaze.

"Oh."

He chuckled at her startled expression, his hand gently rubbing her soft cheek.

"Tell me, my dear, what have I possibly done to deserve such a delectable treat?"

She offered him a pert smile, although her cheeks remained flushed and her eyes dark with bewildered pleasure.

"There are moments when you are quite wonderful, sir," she breathed.

He moved to pull her back close to his body, but with a swift movement she had twirled away and was hurrying toward the house.

A smile curved Anthony's lips as he watched the provocative sway of her hips. The kiss might have been unplanned but it had been utterly enticing. Enticing enough to ensure that he would have another long, restless night, he thought wryly.

Resisting the urge to hurry after her, Anthony forced himself to turn and walk toward the distant stables.

He had crossed past the front of the house and was leaving the courtyard when the sound of footsteps hurrying in his direction had him halting to turn back and discover Lady Broswell forging a determined path in his direction.

With a groan of displeasure he watched the plumes on her bonnet bounce and the skirts of her black bombazine gown flow about her like the sails of a battleship. She was clearly in full pursuit and he would rather hear what she had to say and dismiss her than have her trail him to the stables.

"Mr. Clarke." Lady Broswell smiled as she came to a halt before him, her large bosom heaving from her unaccustomed exertion.

He gave a half bow. "Lady Broswell."

"A lovely day, is it not?"

"Q—quite lovely."

"I had hoped to see you today." Her tone was off-handed, but Anthony did not doubt that she had laid in wait for him the entire morning. He was annoyingly accustomed to matchmaking mamas and their ruthless ploys. "I am planning a small gathering for Friday evening. Quite informal, of course. We should be very honored if you would attend."

"That is very kind, Lady Broswell, but I fear I am quite busy with personal matters."

The thick features tightened with irritation at his smooth dismissal.

"My daughters will be quite disappointed."

"Please offer my apologies. Now if you will excuse me?"

Fully prepared to walk, away Anthony was halted by the preemptory hand laid upon his arm.

"Mr. Clarke."

He glared coldly down his nose until she hastily withdrew her hand. "What is it?"

She hesitated a nervous moment before tilting her chin. "Perhaps it is not my place, but I do feel someone should warn you about Miss Cresswell."

"Indeed?" His silky tone would have warned anyone who knew him that they were traversing dangerous water. Lady Broswell, however, was far too intent on harming Miss Cresswell to take heed of the icy atmosphere.

"A lovely girl, of course, and quite bewitching, but

she is unfortunately indiscriminate in her favors. It is rumored that Mr. Mondale is her current lover."

A sharp, fierce anger surged thorough Anthony. Regardless of the fact that gossip was all too often a pastime for women of Lady Broswell's stamp, to deliberately set out to ruin a young lady's reputation went beyond the pale.

"You are correct, she is a lovely girl," he said, his tone laced with ice. "And quite undeserving of such vile, clearly malicious lies. S—should I hear such rumors circulating in Surrey I assure you that I will be swift to enact my wrath. Do we understand one another, Lady Broswell?"

A shocked silence greeted his overt warning. Then a deep, ugly scarlet flooded the older woman's face.

"Perfectly, Mr. Clarke. Good day."

Turning on her heel, she marched away, every inch of her considerable form quivering with outrage.

Anthony watched her leave with a narrowed gaze.

Gads, but the woman was a harpy. It was little wonder that Rachel was determined to throttle her. At the moment he would gladly do so himself.

Clenching his hands, he turned and continued on his path to the stables. He still had a miracle to create.

Six

Two mornings later Rachel was on the hunt.

Attiring herself in a rose muslin gown that suited the pleasantly warm spring day, she began a thorough search of the house.

It took quite some time to track her quarry to the small conservatory.

Entering the glass and iron room with a few tenacious plants, Rachel crossed toward the bench set close beside a fountain.

It took only a cursory glance to realize that the young maiden had been crying. Rachel felt a prick of sympathy at the reddened eyes and tremble of her soft lips. As she approached, Violet hurriedly tucked her handkerchief out of sight and picked up a discarded piece of linen she had been stitching upon.

Forcing a smile to her lips, Rachel settled on the bench next to her friend.

"Violet, I hoped I would find you."

Violet studiously kept her gaze on the lopsided flower she had printed on the linen. "Good morning, Rachel."

"That is lovely," she murmured, deliberately maneuvering the conversation in the direction she desired.

"Thank you."

"A wedding present for your fiancé?"

She felt Violet shiver at her side. "No. Mr. Wingrove feels that needlework is a frivolous activity. He expects his wife to devote her energies to pleasing her husband and reading books that elevate the mind."

Rachel did not have to pretend her dislike. "Good heavens, what a dreary prig."

"Rachel." Violet glanced up in surprise.

"Well, he is. Forgive me if I offend you, Violet, but I can not imagine that he will make you happy."

Her eyes darkened, but she managed to hold back the ready tears. "Marriage very rarely has anything to do with happiness."

Rachel considered her numerous acquaintances who had wed for position and wealth rather than love. Most of them had already indulged in affairs or were living lives quite separate from their husbands.

"True enough. It is more often a means of retrieving a lost fortune, is it not?"

A sudden surge of painful color stained Violet's countenance. "How did you know?"

Rachel smiled gently. "It is obvious your father has fallen upon hard times. It is equally obvious that you possess nothing but fear and revulsion for your intended."

"It is true," Violet whispered in stricken tones. "Father was always a gamester and after Mother died he only became worse. I begged him to halt, but he always laughed and said that his luck was due to change."

Rachel bit back her harsh words of condemnation. She possessed little sympathy with such self-indulgence. Mr. Carlfield should have concentrated on improving his estate and seeing that his daughter had ensuring a proper dowry, instead of fribbling away his fortune on cards and horses.

"I believe that is the common cry of most gamesters."

"Yes, but his luck did not change and after the Season he was heavily in debt. He realized that he was very close to losing the estate."

"And like any weak man he sought to sacrifice another for his failures rather than accept his responsibilities," she said angrily. "So he hit upon the notion of bartering you to Mr. Wingrove."

"Yes."

Reaching out, Rachel grasped the needlework and tossed it aside, then clasping the ice-cold fingers she regarded her friend with a somber expression.

"You must not do this, Violet. You will be miserable with that ghastly man."

"There is nothing I can do."

"Nonsense. My own mother had been promised to a gentleman she did not love for his title. She was wise enough to elope with my father."

The maiden frowned in a perplexed fashion. "But I have no one who wishes to elope with me."

Rachel schooled her flare of impatience. She must not attempt to consider what she would do in a similar situation. There was no doubt she would have informed her father to his face that she would not be a pawn in his game. Not to mention terrifying any gentleman ridiculous enough to even consider requesting her hand in exchange for money.

Violet possessed a more delicate, more easily swayed spirit. She would always do what was expected of her. It would never occur to her to challenge her father's commands. Not even if it meant tying herself to the wretched Mr. Wingrove.

"What I mean is that she did not allow herself to

be bullied into an unwanted marriage," she said gently. "Tell your father that you refuse to be sacrificed to pay his debts."

Violet gasped in shock at the blunt words. "Oh no. I could not possibly. He would be so angry."

"What is a few angry words when compared to a lifetime with Mr. Wingrove?"

Surprisingly, the pale features hardened at the fierce question. "It would not be just angry words. My father has already threatened to have me turned out if I do not agree to the marriage."

It was Rachel's turn to be shocked. Mr. Carlfield had threatened to toss his own child onto the streets if she did not wed a hideous gentleman old enough to be her own father? It was barbaric. She would dearly love to give the man a proper piece of her mind.

"That is inexcusable," she gritted.

Violet shrugged. "He is terrified of losing everything."

"Then he should have thought of that before tossing away his fortune at the card table."

Clearly of a more sympathetic nature than Rachel, Violet gave a heavy sigh. "It is too late for regrets."

Rachel nibbled her lower lip as she furiously considered what could be done. Certainly she would not stand aside and allow this girl to be bullied into marriage.

And yet, she knew it would be a waste of breath to try and speak with Mr. Carlfield. He clearly possessed nothing but disregard for his only child to have proposed the match in the first place. And nothing could induce her to plea to the mercy of Mr. Wingrove. She did not doubt he would readily punish Violet for Rachel's presumption.

Obviously the only course of action was to snatch Violet from their greedy clutches.

"No, it is not too late," she said in firm tones. "My sister, Sarah, has a town house in London that she has given me. You may live there with me."

The brown eyes abruptly widened. "Truly?"

Rachel chuckled. "Of course. We shall have a grand time."

Just for a moment a glimmer of hope swept over the pale features. Like a condemned prisoner glimpsing a hole in the wall. Then with a pained grimace she gave a slow shake of her head.

"It sounds lovely, but Father would only follow me."

Rachel was not at all frightened by this threat. The law might be on the side of Mr. Carlfield, but she had the cunning of the Devilish Dandy to depend upon. And recalling her father's unusual interest in Violet, she did not doubt for a moment that he would lend his full support.

"You need have no fear of him bothering us in London," she promised confidently. "Uncle Foxworth lives with me. I can assure you that he is more than capable of dealing with your father."

At the mention of Mr. Foxworth the maiden abruptly dropped her gaze. Rachel was intrigued to notice a faint tremble race through her body. It appeared her father was not alone in his fascination.

"Yes, he is a very strong gentleman."

"As well as being thoroughly cunning and clever enough to outwit any gentleman in England," she said dryly.

A silence descended as Violet battled between her well-trained duty to her father and the deep desire to escape the forbidding control of Mr. Wingrove.

"I do not know," she at last whispered. "If I do not wed, what will happen to Father?"

Rachel gave an impatient click of her tongue. "Your father was quite capable of plunging himself into disaster. It is his duty to seek a means of extricating himself."

"It is not so simple."

Rachel once again battled her impatience. She had at least offered the opportunity for escape. It was now up to Violet to decide if she was willing to take the next step.

"Very well." Rachel rose to her feet. "At least think about my offer. I would be quite happy to have you with me."

"I shall." She waited until Rachel had nearly reached the door before she called out softly, "Rachel."

Turning about, Rachel regarded her with raised brows. "Yes?"

"Thank you. I have never known anyone who has been so kind to me."

"Nonsense," Rachel muttered in sudden embarrassment, hurrying from the room before Violet could continue her words of gratitude.

With a shake of her head she moved through the hall toward the front of the house. She deeply pitied Violet. There was no doubt she was browbeaten by her father and terrified of her fiancé. Still, a part of her longed to chide some sense into her.

How could she possibly consider it her duty to rescue her father from financial ruin? If he had not been such a witless buffoon they would not be facing disaster.

Thank goodness her own father had raised her with a strong sense of independence. She would never be the pawn of any man.

She entered the foyer at the same moment a lean, masculine form descended the stairs. Her heart gave a lurch as she met the familiar dark gaze. She had devoted a great deal of thought the previous evening to the blazing kiss they had shared. In truth she had stared at the ceiling long into the night as she had recalled the flood of sensations that had flooded her body.

Until she had encountered Mr. Clarke she had always thought kissing a vastly overrated pastime. Hot lips and groping hands were little more than an annoyance.

Now she realized that such caresses could offer a sweet, darkly dangerous temptation. A temptation far greater than she could ever have dreamed.

"Good morning, Mr. Clarke."

He smiled as he came to a halt before her. "I believe that we have progressed to Anthony, have we not, my dear?"

She hesitated before giving a nod of her head. Common sense might warn her that furthering her intimate contact with this gentleman was a risky gamble, but she had never been one to take the safe path.

"Very well."

Obviously pleased that she had not shied away from his challenge, Anthony stepped closer.

"I had hoped you would be down early this morning."

"Oh? Is there something you desire?"

"Yes. I thought I might visit the local village and hoped you would be willing to accompany me."

Rachel gave a pleased smile. She had already been determined to discover a means of visiting the village. Anthony had saved her from enduring her father's grumbles had he been forced to perform the role of her companion.

"I should like that very much."

"Good. I will join you in the courtyard in a quarter of an hour."

"Very well." She moved to the stairs and made her way calmly to her chamber. Once there, however, she began struggling with the fastenings of her gown, and calling for her maid. "Nellie, I shall need my new carriage gown."

With suitable speed the middle-aged maid was at her side, removing the muslin gown and replacing it with a gown of French gray kerseymere trimmed with white gauze and white satin ribbons. She completed the elegant image with a bonnet of gray velvet with a fall of white lace and black leather half boots. She was uncertain why it was so vital to appear her best for a rustic drive to the village, but she was determined not to leave her chambers until thoroughly satisfied with her appearance.

Pulling a few golden curls from beneath the bonnet to lay against her cheeks, she at last turned back toward her maid.

"A real treat yer look, Miss Cresswell," the woman readily complimented.

"Thank you, Nellie. I hope Mr. Clarke will approve."

The elder woman sniffed. "Have ter be daft not to."

"No, he is not daft." A small smile curved her lips. "But he is very, very elusive."

"Aye, them cagey ones be the most dangerous," the maid said in tones that spoke of years of wisdom.

A faint tingle edged down Rachel's spine. "Yes. They are also the most exciting."

"That be true enough."

"I shall simply have to be more clever than he is." Retrieving her reticule, Rachel turned and left the room, hurrying down the stairs and into the court-yard. She found Anthony waiting for her beside a dashing curricle pulled by a pair of beautifully matched chestnuts. "I hope I have not kept you waiting?"

"Not at all." He allowed his gaze to take an appreciative survey of her trim form. "Are you ready?"

"Yes." She allowed him to lift her into the curricle, then rounding the horses he vaulted into the leather seat and took the reins from the groom. With a flick of his wrists they were on their way. Making herself comfortable in the seat, Rachel prepared to enjoy the lovely day. "What a splendid pair."

"They are a recent p—purchase. I am happy to say they have proven to be quite sound."

She wryly studied his elegant profile. "I can not imagine you are easily fleeced."

"No." He turned to regard her with a shimmering gaze. "I rarely allow surface beauty to sway my opinion. I base my decision upon inner worth."

She arched a brow. "Very noble."

"Indeed." With a chuckle he returned his attention to the narrow lane.

Determined not to be disconcerted, Rachel calmly folded her hands in her lap.

"How does your project go?"

"There are still a few details to be settled."

"May I see it?"

"No," he retorted without apology.

"No?"

"It is to be a s—surprise."

Her lips thinned. If she had ever thought herself irresistible to gentlemen, Anthony was swiftly teaching her that it was nothing more than a vain perception.

"You are very exasperating upon occasion," she informed him sternly.

His heart-stopping smile greeted her reprimand. "And I thought I had progressed to being quite wonderful."

The sharp, vivid memory of their kiss rose to her mind, bringing a swift end to her annoyance. He was wonderful. And intriguing. And utterly fascinating.

Not that she was about to reveal her fascination, she told herself. He was far too confident in his own charm as it was.

"I believe that a woman possesses the prerogative to change her mind," she quipped.

He gave a nod at her direct thrust. "By all means."

Satisfied that she had held her own in the exchange, she regarded him with a curious expression. She deeply desired to probe beneath that enigmatic manner of his. For all the undeniable attraction she felt, she knew precious little about him.

"Tell me of your family."

He appeared startled by her sudden question. "What do you wish to know?"

"Do you have any brothers or sisters?"

"No." His lips twisted in a humorless smile. "I believe my father was suitably disappointed in me without wishing for more offspring."

Rachel stiffened at his soft words. "Disappointed? That is ridiculous."

Anthony shrugged. "My father seeks perfection in all about him. He finds my stutter acutely offensive."

A sharp flare of anger raced through Rachel. "What an arrogant, unlikable ass he must be," she said fiercely.

Anthony gave a startled laugh. "Ah, Rachel, you never fail to amaze me."

"I do not know how you can laugh, Anthony," she

protested with a scowl. "It is unthinkable that a father would not be extremely proud of you. I have met any number of men who claim the title of gentleman, but you are one of the rare few who can claim the title with honor."

His features abruptly softened at her fierce words. "Thank you."

"It is only the truth. And should I encounter your father I shall tell him so myself."

"I have no doubt that you would, my fiery beauty," he said in low tones. "But while I appreciate your readiness to defend me, there is no need. I have learned to accept m—my father's disappointment. Life is too brief to dwell upon those things that I can not alter."

The oddest pang clenched Rachel's heart. Ridiculous, of course. Anthony Clarke was perhaps the last gentleman who needed or desired her sympathy. But the mere thought of a father allowing his young son to grow up feeling unwanted made her teeth clench.

"You are far more forgiving than I should be."

He grimaced wryly. "It was not always so. I devoted years attempting to prove to my father that I was worthy of his admiration. I excelled in school, invested my allowance until I had acquired a fortune, and I purchased the finest estate in the county. It was never enough. In his eyes I w—will always be flawed. I at last realized that I desired his admiration only because I did not admire myself. Once I accepted I was worthy, I no longer needed his approval."

The sudden image of Lady Broswell rose to Rachel's mind. She could not deny that a small portion of her desire for revenge was the knowledge that her aunt considered her far inferior to herself. It was a thorn that refused to be dislodged. But unlike Anthony, she did not desire to ignore the slights and insults she had endured over the years. She wanted to force Lady Broswell to admit that she was as respectable and well-bred as her own daughters.

"It was his duty to love and cherish you. Why else do we have a family?"

He slowed their brisk pace as they came to a corner. "A lovely sentiment, but rarely a reality. Families are willed upon us whether we wish them or not."

She grimaced. "Yes."

"The more troublesome ones are best forgotten."

"Sometimes they make such a desire impossible."

He shot her a speculative glance, but before he could ask the obvious questions trembling upon his lips, they were coming into the outskirts of the small village.

"I believe we have arrived," he murmured.

Rachel gazed about with interest. Not that there was much to see. A handful of half-timbered buildings lined one edge of the narrow road while a solid inn with a wooden sign proclaiming it to be the FOX AND GRAPES dominated the far side. Farther down she could detect what she supposed to be a blacksmith and farther along a small gothic church and vicarage.

It was a quaint-enough sight, she acknowledged, with a gaggle of geese crossing the green and several young boys laughing as they kicked a ball down the street and then went rushing after it. Not even the locals who halted to openly ogle the smart carriage and elegant strangers managed to destroy the bucolic peace.

But she had not traveled to the village to appreciate the sights. She briefly feared her journey had been in vain.

"Goodness. There is not much to choose from."

Pulling the horses to a halt, Anthony gazed at her with curiosity. "Are you seeking anything in particular?"

"Yes. A dressmaker."

The dark brows rose in surprise, his gaze traveling over her expertly tailored gown.

"Would it not be wiser to wait for a new gown until you return to London? Any local seamstress is unlikely to possess the skill you are accustomed to."

She gave a decisive shake of her head. "I fear I can not wait. I must have the gown by the end of next week."

"For the ball?" he demanded in disbelief.

"Yes."

He studied her innocent expression for a long moment. "What are you plotting, Rachel?"

Enjoying the sensation that she had cleverly turned the tables on him, she merely smiled.

"I do not know what you mean."

"You would not entrust something as important as your ball gown to the dubious talents of a country dressmaker," he retorted in impatient tones.

"I did not say that the gown was for me."

Her soft words took him aback and his mouth opened to demand an explanation. Then a sudden realization hit him and the dark eyes smoldered with a fire of pleasure.

"I do not suppose this gown will be blue with white lace upon it?" he demanded, referring to the wish Julia had made for just such a gown.

With a deliberate effort she acquired her most aloof manner.

"That, sir, is a secret."

He tilted back his head to give a warm, delighted laugh. "You know, Rachel, there are moments when you are quite wonderful yourself."

Seven

Rachel was pleasantly surprised by the local seamstress. Although naturally intimidated to have a lady of Quality in her modest shop, she was eager to please and swift to grasp Rachel's notions of a suitable gown for Julia. Together they chose a satin material in a shade of blue that would match the girl's eyes and a lovely Brussels lace that would trim the hem of the gown with blue ribbons. There was a hint of panic when Rachel informed the woman that she would need the gown in less than a fortnight, but a charming smile and handful of coins had soon eased the momentary troubles.

Satisfied that the young girl would be vastly pleased with her new gown, Rachel strolled through the village green and seated herself on a bench to wait for Anthony.

Although the breeze still held a hint of winter, it was a lovely afternoon. She sucked in a deep breath, inhaling the scent of baking bread and tender grass.

It was odd.

She had always considered such pastoral settings tediously dull. What lady of sophistication could discover any amusement in empty meadows and grazing cows? Today, however, she felt a sense of contentment as she allowed the sweet peace to settle about her.

For the moment she did not miss her usual crowd of anxious admirers. Or even the mad rush from one event to another. London seemed far away and she was happy for it to be so.

Not that she intended to dwell upon her queer sense of satisfaction, she acknowledged ruefully. She did not wish to ponder her sharp, almost fierce desire to help poor Julia. Or her deep fascination with Anthony Clarke.

Neither suited the carefree existence that she so enjoyed. If she truly allowed herself to consider her peculiar behavior she would no doubt be more than a bit disturbed.

It was far better to simply ignore the whispers of warnings that stirred in the back of her mind.

Nearly another hour passed before Anthony's elegant form at last could be seen striding down the lane with a heavy bag tucked under one arm. Rachel rose to her feet, unable to deny a jolt of excitement at the sight of him.

What was it about this gentleman that sent frissons of pleasure racing through her body? she mused.

Certainly he possessed a commanding form and handsome features. And there was an undeniable charm to his self-possessed confidence. But she had encountered men far more handsome. And flirted with the most charming men in all of England and Europe.

And yet it was only Anthony Clarke who had managed to teach her the dangerous temptation of desire.

With a faint shrug at the mystery she moved to where Anthony was storing the bag beneath the seat of the carriage. At her approach he flashed her a smile and promptly moved to help her climb onto the padded seat.

"Was your trip successful?" he inquired as he joined her and set the restless team into motion.

Rachel briefly imagined Julia's pleasure when she presented her with the gown.

"I believe so. And yours?"

He deftly urged the horses to a greater speed as they left the small village behind.

"I make progress."

She flashed him a frown of amused exasperation. "You are determined to keep your project a secret?"

"Yes."

Rachel ignored the urge to coax the truth from him. She had already discovered this gentleman could not be easily cajoled or manipulated. He would do as he pleased regardless of her supposedly irresistible charm.

"You were gone a very long time," she said instead.

As if sensing her inner thoughts, he smiled in a knowing manner.

"I must apologize. The local tanner was a rather gregarious soul who was quite determined to instruct me on the glorious history of Surrey."

She gave a lift of her brows. "It must have been fascinating."

"Actually it was, rather," he surprised her by admitting firmly. "For instance, he informed me that Edward the Second often visited a nearby manor to indulge his fascination with jousts. Unfortunately his visits came to an end when the owner of the manor was beheaded."

She grimaced at the gruesome tale. "Charming."

He chuckled. "What do you find offensive? The jousting or the beheading?"

"Both are barbaric."

"Oh, I d—do not know. There is something rather romantic about the chivalrous knights plunging into competition, all to win the heart of their fair maiden."

"My heart would be more readily won by the gentleman with enough wits not to risk his neck in such a foolish manner," she said dryly. "I find nothing romantic in dented armor and bruised backsides."

"And you claim me to be the only overly logical one," he teased.

She shrugged. "I can not conceive of you being compelled to prove your vanity by knocking another off his horse."

"Perhaps not." He flashed her a glance. "Although it might be worth the effort if you were willing to tend to my bruised backside."

"Sir."

He gave a pleased laugh. "Very well, perhaps you will prefer the tale of a village near here called Merstham where the tanner claimed that in 1851 an invading Danish army was retreating from a lost battle only to be met by the local women who attacked them with sticks and whatever else they could lay their hands on, including frying pans. The poor Danish were no match for the infuriated women."

A smile curved her lips. "Yes, I do like that story."

"I thought you might. You can be quite b—bloodthirsty, my dear."

"It is not that."

"Oh?"

"No, I have always known women could be quite capable when given the opportunity," she retorted in deliberately smug tones. "It is only men who persist in believing they are somehow incapable of shouldering responsibility."

He slowed the team so he could properly study her challenging expression.

"And what responsibilities would those be?"

She did not hesitate. "Controlling our own fortunes, buying property, choosing our futures rather than being at the whim of a gentleman."

"Egads." He gave a choked laugh. "I can imagine no lady less likely to be at the whim of a gentleman, my dear."

"No, I am fortunate to possess a father who values my independence," she readily agreed, ignoring his obvious amusement. "Other women are not nearly so fortunate. Just consider Violet being forced into marriage with a gentleman she detests, all to save her father from a ruin of his own making."

" 'Tis unfortunate, I must admit."

The memory of Violet's haunted eyes made Rachel's hands clench in her lap.

"It should be a crime," she said, wishing she could personally haul Mr. Carlfield and Mr. Wingrove to the nearest gallows.

He arched his brows in surprise at her fervent tones. "You are not a radical by any chance, are you, Rachel?"

"It is all so ghastly unfair."

"Maidens are not the only ones f—forced into marriage for reasons other than love."

She could not deny his logic. She had only to consider Lord Newell and the distasteful pressure being applied on him to wed Miss Hamlin. Still the situations were not entirely equal.

"Perhaps, but at least a gentleman possesses the means of supporting himself if he chooses to disregard his family's commands."

"Do you truly believe Violet capable of supporting

herself even given the opportunity?" he demanded in disbelief.

It did seem a ludicrous notion, she had to admit. Violet was far too timid and uncertain of herself to face a life without the protection of wealth. She would faint in horror at the mere thought of forging into the world on her own. But Rachel could not conceive that she would be any less frightened and miserable shoved into the arms of Mr. Wingrove.

"Desperation will allow one to accomplish things one never dreamed possible," she said softly.

"Violet would be lost without someone to care for her, as you are well aware. She does not possess your spirit or your courage."

Rachel felt a prick of annoyance. He had not seen the horror in the wide eyes.

"You can not wish her to marry that obnoxious bore?"

"No, but it must be V—Violet who chooses to end her engagement," he said in firm tones. "Would I be any less a bully than her father to persuade her to turn Mr. Wingrove away?"

She opened her mouth, then heaved a reluctant sigh. "Must you always be so sensible?"

The dark eyes flashed in amusement. "I fear so. It is a great fault, I will admit."

"A fault, indeed," she mourned in sympathy. "But I am generous enough to overlook such terrible flaws in your character."

"How very kind of you, my dear."

"Yes, indeed."

He chuckled at her air of self-sacrifice, then abruptly changed the conversation.

"I have told you of my family, but you have told me little of yours."

She was startled by his interest. There were few

among society daring enough to question her directly about the Devilish Dandy.

"What do you wish to know?"

"What was your childhood like?"

She paused before giving a wry grimace. "Exciting, unpredictable, and occasionally frightening when we feared Father was about to be discovered," she surprised herself by answering honestly. She rarely revealed anything but the most flippant details of her past. "It was also rather lonely because we never truly had a home. Thank goodness for Sarah and Emma."

"Your sisters?"

"Yes."

His gaze swept over her delicate features. "Are they as beautiful and daring as you?"

Rachel smiled as she thought of her sisters. "They are certainly beautiful and I suppose daring in their own ways. Sarah raised both Emma and me after my mother died and then defied convention by opening a school in the worst neighborhood in London. I do not doubt that she will continue to run it even though she will soon be Lady Chance. As for Emma"—she paused as she recalled their somewhat stormy relationship—"she refused to accept help from anyone and became a companion to Lady Hartshore before she won the heart of the Earl of Hartshore. I used to tease her unmercifully about her stuffy nature and refusal to enjoy life. She hated being the daughter of the Devilish Dandy. Now she simply sparkles with happiness."

"You sound almost envious," he retorted.

Rachel gave a blink. Until this moment she had not considered she might feel a trace of jealousy at her sisters' good fortune.

"Perhaps I am a bit," she slowly confessed. "Both

Sarah and Emma have found gentlemen who respect and adore them. I do not doubt for a moment they will be extraordinarily happy."

"And yet you c—claim you have no interest in having a husband or family," he reminded her in soft tones.

She didn't, she sternly assured herself. Her life was delightful as it was. Exciting, unencumbered, and without the restrictions of a husband or children. Those small pangs when she viewed her sisters with their devoted fiancés were easily dismissed. As were the moments of loneliness that struck without warning.

"I fear that my sisters have discovered a rare breed of gentleman." She deliberately lightened her tone. "They will not be required to bow to their husbands' commands or be treated to an endless line of mistresses. They will be cherished as they deserve to be."

"You believe only two gentlemen in all of England possess such qualities?" he demanded with a hint of exasperation.

The hazel eyes glinted with pleasure at having ruffled his cool self-command.

"Well, perhaps there are one or two others," she graciously conceded. "What of you? Do you intend to wed?"

He turned onto a path that wandered through a wide meadow. A covey of quail surged into the air, calling their disapproval as they flew toward the blue sky.

"As you have so kindly pointed out, I should make a ghastly husband," he at last retorted. "I rarely enjoy society, I often disappear for hours upon end to my workroom, and I prefer a good book to dancing the waltz."

She studied his elegant profile. "Surely you must produce an heir?"

"Thankfully my father's brother has managed to produce a prodigious gaggle of children. He has relieved me of any duty to carry on the family line."

"So you intend to remain a bachelor?"

A decidedly wicked expression settled on his countenance. "I suppose the proper maiden might lure me down the aisle. She would have to be quite out of the ordinary, of course."

"Out of the ordinary?"

"Yes, indeed. She must be beautiful, charming, gracious, and independent enough not to demand my constant attention."

"Are there any other requirements?" she demanded in dry tones.

He pretended to consider the matter. "She must be sweet-tempered, intelligent, blessed with a sense of humor, and possess a kind heart."

"Fah." She gave a reluctant laugh at his ridiculous demands. "I think you had best attempt to create this model of virtue in your workroom. You shall never discover a mere maiden who can meet your demands."

He appeared unperturbed by her confident disbelief in perfection.

"Oh, I do not know. My m—mother was such a woman."

Rachel recalled his words to Julia of how his mother had explained his faint stutter. "Kissed by an angel." She must be a wonderful woman indeed, she acknowledged.

"Are you still close to her?"

"Very close," he murmured, his tender tone making her heart give an odd flop.

"I should have liked to know my mother," she admitted with a wistful sigh. "Father says she was very gentle and ready to love whomever she met. He also said her laughter could fill an entire room with joy."

He reached out to brush her cheek before returning his hand to the reins.

"You most certainly inherited her laughter."

It was perhaps the greatest compliment she had ever received.

"Thank you," she said softly.

"Your father never remarried?"

Rachel widened her eyes in surprise at the unexpected question.

"I do not believe many women would desire to tie themselves to the Devilish Dandy, even if he does possess the charm of Lucifer. Besides, he still loves my mother."

"Do you miss him?"

"Of course," she replied cautiously, all too aware that this gentleman was far too intelligent to be easily fooled. "But I realize that he can never return to England. It would be far too dangerous."

"That must be very difficult for you."

She shrugged. "I have my sisters and Uncle Foxworth."

"Ah, Uncle Foxworth. A most unusual gentleman."

"Yes." She covertly studied his bland expression, wondering if he already suspected her uncle was not quite what he seemed. "Do you like him?"

"He is intriguing." He tossed her a wry grin. "Although I should never wish to purchase a horse from him."

"A wise choice," she congratulated dryly.

"You know, you f—fascinate me, my dear."

Relieved to have the conversation turned from her father, Rachel met his dark gaze.

"Why?"

"Most maidens would be horrified to possess a father who is a thief and an uncle who consorts with a gossip-plagued prince."

"I love them," she said without hesitation. "I would not trade them for a hundred so-called respectable gentlemen."

"They are fortunate to have earned your loyalty."

"Earned?" She wrinkled her brow at his strange choice of words. "They had no need to earn my loyalty. They are my family."

He fell silent at her simple words, his expression suddenly remote.

Unwilling to disturb his inner thoughts, Rachel watched as they pulled into the drive leading to Carlfield Manor. In only a few moments they had swept past the towering oaks and were pulling to a halt in the courtyard.

A groom ran forward to take the reins as Anthony leaped to the ground and rounded the carriage to help Rachel alight. Just for a moment his hands lingered on her slender waist, then with a reluctant sigh he stepped back.

"I wish to thank you for accompanying me today."

"I enjoyed myself," she retorted with all honesty. She had enjoyed herself. Far more than a simple trip to the local village warranted.

"As did I," he said warmly.

There was a moment's pause as Rachel battled the urge to demand if he was about to once again disappear to the stables to dabble with his mysterious project. The lazy glint in his dark eyes warned her that that was precisely what he was expecting her to do. Instead she forced herself to offer him an airy smile.

"I wish you luck on your project. Perhaps I will see you at dinner."

She whirled away before he could speak and with her head held high she moved toward the open front door. She was not about to reveal just how badly she wished to plead to be at his side.

Reaching beneath the seat to retrieve the bag he had received from the tanner, Anthony walked toward the nearby stables. A smile curved his lips at the challenge that had sparkled in the hazel eyes as Rachel had turned away.

She was as spirited as she was beautiful. A heady combination. But there was more to her than just lovely curves and a swift tongue, he acknowledged.

He had already discovered that she possessed a kind heart just by her reaction to Julia. But he had been strangely moved by her bold declaration of loyalty to her father.

She was a woman who loved without judgment. Who gave her heart and loyalty without condemning another for their frailties.

Perhaps for most gentlemen her open attachment to a known thief would cause a reasonable distress. The undoubted scandal attached to her name was only exasperated by her refusal to appear suitably horrified by her connection to the Devilish Dandy. But for Anthony it was a quality he deeply admired. He had endured his fill of those who offered their love only to impose impossible conditions to maintain their affection.

Entering the shadows of the stables, Anthony halted as a tall, lean form stepped forward. He felt a flicker of surprise as he met the glittering green gaze.

"Mr. Foxworth," he murmured.

The older gentleman gave a faint nod of his head. "Mr. Clarke."

"Are you riding today?"

"Actually, I was waiting for you."

Although Anthony had already suspected as much, he lifted a dark brow. "Indeed?"

"Yes, I particularly wished to speak with you in private."

"About what?"

Foxworth stroked a faint scar on his cheek. "I believe you have been out riding with my niece?"

Anthony's expression became guarded, wondering where the wily man was about to lead him.

"We visited the local village."

"She is a lovely girl, is she not?"

"Quite lovely."

"She is also headstrong and dangerously impulsive," Mr. Foxworth continued, studying Anthony with an unnerving intensity. "She rarely considers the consequences before she plunges into a situation."

Anthony could not prevent his wry smile. "Yes, I h—have noticed such tendencies."

"Then you will understand if I am rather protective of her."

Ah, so he was about to receive a stern warning, Anthony acknowledged with a flare of amused disbelief. An odd thought for a gentleman far more accustomed to having young maidens tossed at his feet.

"Certainly," he agreed in mild tones.

"I should not like to see her reckless nature lead her to anything she might later have reason to regret."

Anthony arched a dark brow. "Are you inquiring whether I intend to be an honorable gentleman?"

Mr. Foxworth abruptly smiled. "I did not intend to be quite so blunt, but yes."

It was not often that Anthony found his honor questioned and he discovered that he did not particularly care for the experience.

"I consider Miss Cresswell an extraordinary maiden who deserves all the respect due to her. I would never compromise her innocence or her integrity."

The green gaze never wavered. "And what of her heart?"

"It will never be my intention to hurt her."

"Unfortunately it rarely is intentional. That does not make the pain less. Especially for a girl who leads with her heart."

Anthony could not deny the truth in his words. Although Rachel tried very hard to give the image of a shallow, hardened flirt, she was very vulnerable beneath the flamboyant charm. Far more vulnerable than even he had suspected.

"I s—shall keep that in mind."

"See that you do."

His warning delivered, the older gentleman turned to negligently stroll from the stables. Anthony watched with a strange sense of unease.

He did not particularly care to be warned off like he was a lecherous cad. Especially by a gentleman he suspected was far from a saint. On the other hand he had to admit his determined pursuit of Miss Cresswell was enough to stir the suspicion of any proper guardian.

Even worse, he could hardly assure Mr. Foxworth of his intentions, when he had no notion of what his intentions were.

Certainly he wanted to seduce Rachel. Whenever she was near he nearly trembled with the effort to keep himself from pulling her into his arms and drowning in her sweetness. And his nights . . . Gads, he had never ached with such fierce need.

But he had not lied to Mr. Foxworth when he had assured him that he would always treat Rachel with respect. He did not seduce virgins and leave them to their shattered fates. And he did not doubt for a moment she was utterly innocent.

So where did that leave him?

Frustrated, certainly.

Puzzled.

Tantalized.

Distracted.

And yet, at this moment he would not be anywhere else in the world.

"Sir, did you get what you be needing?"

With a blink Anthony realized that he had been joined by the young groom who had happily agreed to help with his current project.

He readily shoved aside his tangled thoughts. What was the point in brooding about questions that had no answers? It was far better to tackle the problems that could be solved.

"I believe so." He held up his bag. "Shall we get to work?"

Eight

Standing in the shadows of the salon, Anthony surveyed the numerous guests as they chatted and flirted with casual ease.

It had been the same every evening for the past week.

Mr. Carlfield was clearly determined to celebrate in lavish style his good fortune in landing a wealthy son-in-law. There was rarely a moment when the house was not filled with visitors enjoying luncheons, dinners, musicales, and card parties. Under normal circumstances Anthony would long ago have fled to the quiet peace of his London town house. He intensely disliked the constant need to make polite conversation at every turn.

But despite his discomfort his bags remained unpacked. And he did not have to look far to discover the reason for his unusual forbearance.

Leaning against the faded paneling, Anthony allowed his gaze to linger on the golden-haired beauty that had so mysteriously lured him to Surrey.

No, he swiftly corrected his inane thoughts. There was nothing mysterious about his arrival in Surrey.

His blood quickened as he studied the elegant profile, then lowered to the delicious curves nicely revealed by the emerald silk gown cut to emphasize the luscious fullness of her bosom. He had followed her because he could not help himself.

The only mystery was what he intended to do now that he was here.

A faint smile curved his lips as he watched the object of his fascination stifle a yawn. At the moment she was surrounded by a gaggle of elder matrons who were fiercely debating the traditions involved in making the perfect wedding. It was a debate that had raged for a better part of an hour and Anthony was not surprised when he noticed Rachel begin to edge away from the clucking women. He patiently waited until she had made good her escape and settled on a far sofa with obvious relief. Unlike most young maidens, she did not devote her life to the grand dream of becoming wed. Indeed, she was rather annoying in her desire never to be chained to the bonds of a gentleman. He had known it would be only a matter of time before she sought peace from the incessant discussion.

Nonchalantly pushing himself from the wall, Anthony strolled across the room and boldly sat next to her on the sofa.

"You appear somewhat bored, my dear," he teased lightly.

She wrinkled her nose in disgust. "Such a fuss over a mere wedding."

"There are certain customs to be observed. Most of them have been around hundreds of years."

The hazel eyes flashed at his calm words. "Are you an expert on weddings by chance?"

"Just well read," he retorted, ignoring her deliberate barb as he reached out to grasp her left hand. "For instance did you know that we place the wedding ring on the third finger because the Greeks thought it directly connected to the heart by the 'Vein of Love'?" He traced a light path from the palm of her hand up to her elbow, reveling in the unmistakable shiver he felt race through her body. "Or that many Roman rings were carved with two clasped hands to represent love and commitment?"

Seemingly as indifferent to the covert glances being tossed in their directions as himself, Rachel leaned forward. Anthony deeply inhaled the rose scent of her skin.

"That is very romantic."

"It is also thought that the tradition of the Best Man comes from the days when a man would capture his bride from a neighboring village and would take his most formidable friend along for security. That was also the reason the bride was placed on his left during the ceremony. He could never be certain when he would need his sword hand free to battle off an attack of angry relatives."

She gave a shake of her head. "Now that is not nearly as romantic."

"Would you like me to explain the traditions of the honeymoon?" he asked softly, continuing to stroke the soft inner skin of her elbow.

Her eyes darkened. "No, I think that I have been educated enough for one evening."

"A p—pity. It is quite fascinating."

"Yes, I suppose it might be." She paused then she drew in a deep breath. "Do you know, it has grown quite warm in here."

He was not slow to pick up her hint and a ready heat flowed through his lower body. He wanted nothing more than to whisk her away from the swelling crowd. It had been far too long since he had held her in his arms. But the knowledge that Mr. Foxworth was currently regarding them with a narrowed gaze made him hesitate.

He did not fear the older man, but he did respect his right to be concerned for his niece's welfare.

"I would offer to take you out for a breath of air, but I have been specifically warned to behave with proper restraint in your presence."

Her brow creased in puzzlement. "Whatever do you mean?"

"Your uncle was quite clear that I am not to break your heart."

"Ah." She abruptly chuckled. "He is very protective."

"Yes. He does not realize just how very elusive that heart of yours is."

Her gaze lowered to where his fingers absently stroked her skin.

"Do you wish to break my heart?"

"Certainly not," he denied in firm tones. "I would never harm you. But I do wonder if that specific organ can be reached."

"Like you, it would take someone very special," she said softly.

"Ah." He closely studied the lowered lashes, the slender nose, and the satin softness of her lips. He realized that he very much wished to discover what sort of gentleman would tempt her to toss aside her proudly flaunted independence. "And what are your requirements?"

She deliberately paused, as if considering her answer. "He would have to be handsome, of course."

"Of course."

"And of a romantic disposition."

"Is that all?"

"Certainly not." Her gaze lifted to regard him with a steady gaze. "He would have to be intelligent and strong, but he could not attempt to treat me as a witless child. And he would have to adore me."

The heady scent of roses was quickly going to his head. "Who would not?"

"And he could not constantly forget my presence in favor of his workroom," she concluded with open delight at besting him.

He slowly smiled. The mere notion of any gentleman forgetting her presence was ludicrous. Were she in his house the only reason he would be in his workroom would be if she were with him. Perhaps assisting him with his current invention. Or better still, leading him to the small sofa he kept in the corner . . .

With an effort he forced his thoughts from the dangerous images.

"You expect a gentleman who will dance constant attendance upon you?" he demanded in light tones.

She shrugged. "I would not wish to be ignored."

Anthony gave a slow shake of his head. He knew that her words were designed merely to torment him.

"There is a v—vast difference between being ignored and smothering someone with attention. I do not believe you would care for a gentleman who would demand to be always at your side or who would complain if he did not know precisely where you were every moment of the day. An independent woman would soon chaff beneath such a tight bridle."

She regarded him with wry annoyance, unable to deny the truth of his words.

"I do not believe I wish to be likened to a horse."

"You know that I am right."

"You think you know me very well."

He laughed softly at the hint of pique in her tone. "On the contrary. You remain a tempting enigma. I do, however, possess enough sense to realize that a high-spirited minx would not wish to be caged by any man."

Her chin tilted. "And you would be driven to distraction by a sweetly demur chit who preferred you in your workroom rather than in her company."

Ah, so his earlier words had pricked a nerve, he thought with a flare of satisfaction. It was an intriguing discovery.

"Perhaps."

Rachel felt her heart quiver as Anthony leaned slowly forward. Over the past few days she had missed these tantalizing encounters. With so many guests it was nearly impossible to find a moment alone with him. And, of course, he continued to be aggravatingly elusive, disappearing without warning to the stables or the nearby village.

She discovered herself searching for him each time she walked into a room. And when he wasn't there she felt a sharp pang of loneliness that was nearly frightening in its intensity.

Never had a mere man managed to intrude so deeply into her thoughts.

Her breath caught as his gaze lowered to her lips, then the loud booming voice of the butler echoed through the room, making his elegant countenance suddenly tighten with annoyance.

"It appears we have more guests," he said in even tones.

Rachel glanced toward the door, where Lady Broswell stood with her two daughters and Lord Newell. It was precisely what she had desired when she came to Surrey. She had known that Lord Newell was bound to make an appearance with his godmother and soon-to-be fiancé. It was the perfect opportunity to prove how easily she could lure the young gentleman from their side.

But rather than elation at having an opportunity to further her revenge, Rachel could not deny a stab of disappointment that her moment alone with Anthony appeared to be at an end.

"Lady Broswell," she murmured.

"And your devoted admirer from the opera."

"Yes. Lord Newell."

The dark eyes narrowed. "It pleases you that he prefers your charms to those of Miss Hamlin?"

Her expression became defensive at the edge of reproach in his tone. He could not possibly understand. No one could understand.

"It provides a certain satisfaction."

His lips twisted as he rose to his feet. "Then I shall leave you to your game."

She opened her mouth to beg him to stay. She did not want to be left on her own. Not even for the sake of furthering her revenge. Then realizing her absurd weakness, she forced herself to swallow the hasty words.

Good heavens, she was Miss Rachel Cresswell, she sternly reminded herself. She had no need to plead for a man's attentions. Any man's attentions.

Forcing an indifferent smile, she watched him stroll back to the far shadows of the room.

He would never suspect the sharp pang that shot through her heart at his sudden defection.

The stiff smile remained intact even as she realized that Lord Newell was hurrying in her direction. This was the reason she had come to Surrey, she forced herself to acknowledge. Not to be bedeviled by Anthony Clarke.

"Miss Cresswell." Lord Newell readily settled beside her, appearing rather ridiculous in a burgundy striped coat and a fussy cravat that no doubt took an hour to tie. Not at all like Anthony, who preferred a simple elegance, she inanely thought. Of course, Lord Newell was far too scrawny to appear anything but absurd without his padding and frills. "I could not believe my fortune when I learned you were a guest here."

"Lord Newell, how pleasant to see you again."

His gaze avidly devoured the white expanse of her bosom before reluctantly raising to meet her hazel eyes.

"You look beautiful. Like an angel fallen from heaven."

"How kind of you," she forced herself to murmur, inwardly wondering if gentlemen were taught such mundane compliments along with Latin and Greek in school. She had lost count of how many occasions she had heard those precise words. "And of course you are as handsome as ever. Is that a new coat?"

He instantly preened in delight. "I say, do you like it?"

"It is quite eye-catching."

Predictably missing the irony in her words, he ran a hand over the smooth material.

"Cost a wretched fortune, but well worth every quid."

"Does that mean your mother has halted her threats to have your allowance brought to an end?"

"Gads, no." His smile dimmed. "The old Tartar is determined to have me leg-shackled by the end of the year."

Rachel deliberately glanced toward where Lady Broswell and her two-long faced daughters were glaring daggers at her.

"What will you do?"

"What can I do?" he demanded in plaintive tones. "I shall have to wed the chit."

She slowly returned her attention to the boy at her side. "You could always refuse."

"Refuse?" He appeared deeply shocked by the mere suggestion. "You do not know my mother. She is contrary enough to end my allowance. It will still be three years before I will have control of my inheritance."

Rachel lifted a golden brow. "So, you will wed Miss Hamlin even though you do not care for her?"

He shrugged his indifference. "It is expected and I must marry someday. One maiden is as good as another."

Until that moment Rachel's sympathies had lain entirely with this gentleman. The mere thought of being bullied into marriage by Lady Broswell was utterly repulsive. Now she felt a faint, unwelcome stab of pity for Mary. She would soon be tied to this weak, self-absorbed gentleman, who did not even possess a morsel of affection for her.

With an effort she thrust aside the notion. She would not allow herself to weaken.

"And I thought you claimed that I was quite special," she teased in flirtatious tones.

"Good Lord, I was not referring to you, Miss Cresswell," he swiftly denied, anxious to assure her that he intended no insult. "You are a bright shining star. A vision that takes my breath away."

"My lord, you shall quite turn my head."

"I wish that I could," he said wistfully, leaning far too close. "May I call on you tomorrow?"

Rachel briefly considered Lady Broswell's response to the thought of her prospective son-in-law charging from her home to be with her hated niece. She would be furious, of course, and deeply humiliated that Lord Newell obviously preferred Rachel to her daughter.

It was precisely what she wanted.

But even as a part of her urged her to agree to his request, her gaze sought out the masculine form standing so still in a far corner of the room. She did not want to waste her day fending off the advances of this awkward boy, she abruptly realized. Even if it did mean infuriating her aunt. There would be any number of opportunities to tease Lady Broswell.

"I do not believe Lady Broswell would care for the notion," she at last retorted.

"There is no need for her to know."

"This is not London, my lord. I fear gossip would travel very swiftly through the countryside."

His lips dropped in a petulant fashion at the truth in her words.

"I suppose you are right." He heaved a sigh. "How I wish I could speak with you alone."

"Is there something of a private nature you wish to discuss with me?"

He reached out to grasp her hand in a near-painful grip. "There is so much. Things that I can not speak of with others so near."

Rachel determinedly pulled her maltreated fingers free, consumed with impatience with the overeager gentleman.

"My lord, you must think of your poor fiancée."

"Fah. As long as I wed her, she will not concern herself with my interests."

Realizing that there was only one certain method of ridding herself of his presence, she deliberately glanced at the Broswell clan, who were decidedly flushed as they stared in their direction.

"She does not appear disinterested at the moment. Indeed, I would hazard a guess that she is quite annoyed."

As expected, Lord Newell cast a hasty glance toward his soon-to-be fiancée. He seemed to shrink as he met Mary's gaze. He no doubt realized he was bound to endure a severe tongue-lashing for his betrayal.

"Blast. I suppose I should return to her side," he muttered, rising to his feet. "I shall have to speak with you later, my dear."

He hurried away without a backward glance and Rachel heaved a faint sigh. She had never been more relieved that she had been born into the scandalous side of the family. Her father would never pressure her into a cold, loveless relationship. He cared far more that she was happy than smothered in the heavy expectations of society.

It was perhaps the greatest gift he had ever given her.

Absently watching Lady Broswell furiously whispering in Lord Newell's ear, Rachel failed to note the elegant gentleman circling the room to stand directly behind her. It was only when a slender finger stroked a feather-light caress down the back of her neck that she realized Anthony had returned.

She shivered as her body immediately reacted to his proximity.

"W—well, my dearest, if you hoped to infuriate Lady Broswell I believe you have succeeded."

Knowing that she had been far kinder than she had intended to be and that it was entirely this gentleman's fault, she refused to apologize.

"I can hardly be responsible for the behavior of Lord Newell."

"You are thoroughly responsible, as you well know. You have bewitched the poor sod."

"I have been polite."

He gave a low chuckle, his fingers still trailing a disturbing path along the curve of her neck.

"I am not one of your witless admirers, Rachel.

I can tell when a woman is encouraging a young gentleman."

She shrugged, not about to reveal that she had not been nearly as encouraging as she could have been. Lord Newell would still be at her side if she had not sent him on his way.

"You are at liberty to believe what you will."

There was a pause before she heard him heave a faint sigh.

"Ah, I do not wish to argue. Do you still find the room overly warm?"

All thoughts of Lord Newell fled as a tingle of anticipation rushed through her. She very much wanted to be alone with this man.

"What of my uncle?"

"He seems to have disappeared," he said in low tones. "Shall we take a turn on the veranda?"

"Very well."

She rose to her feet, waiting for Anthony to round the sofa and claim her arm. Together they moved through the guests and at last through the door that led to the veranda. Rachel drew in a deep breath as the dark peace settled about them.

It was lovely to be away from the chattering guests and baleful glares of Lady Broswell. And, of course, it was even more lovely to be close enough to Anthony to feel the heat of his body surround her.

A familiar shiver surged through her and Anthony glanced down in concern.

"Are you cold?"

"No," she hurriedly denied, not wishing the moment to end. "It is very mild."

"I believe that spring is attempting to make it's presence known."

"Yes."

Without warning he came to a halt, his hands

reaching out to grasp her shoulders and turn her to face him. By the silvery moonlight Rachel watched as he studied her upturned countenance and slender form with thrilling urgency.

"You know, I have always thought of you as a woman of sunshine, so bright and warm with life, but you appear quite provocative by the light of the moon."

Rachel's breath became unsteady as she met the smoldering dark gaze.

"Why, Anthony, was that a compliment?"

"M—merely an observation. I leave empty compliments to rogues and schoolboys."

She stepped closer, her heart thundering in her chest. "Do you have any other observations?"

He smiled as his hands moved from her shoulders to trail his fingers along the line of her plunging neckline.

"I suppose that I could tell you that your skin possesses the purity of a rare pearl and that your eyes have been kissed with gold dust. Or that your lips are perfectly formed to fit my own and your body so sweetly curved that I ache to feel it pressed beneath me."

Rachel was trembling from head to toe as those seeking fingers plunged beneath the silk of her bodice to caress the soft curve of her breast.

"Oh."

Clearly sensing her rising passion, Anthony slowly lowered his head to claim her lips in a branding kiss. Rachel tilted her head back, readily allowing him access to her mouth. He groaned as he hungrily tasted her desire, his hands cupping the fullness of her breasts.

Rachel grasped his arms, afraid she might fall to her knees as a sharp, unbearably sweet pleasure flooded through her. Gads, she felt as if she were drowning in the sensations she had never even dreamed existed.

With an impatient urgency his mouth moved from her throbbing lips to sear a path over her cheek and down the line of her neck. He nuzzled the frantic pulse at the base of her throat and Rachel moaned in approval.

"I did not know a kiss could feel like this," she said in broken tones.

His soft laugh brushed her sensitive skin. "Is that good or bad?"

"I am not entirely certain," she admitted.

He trailed his lips over her collarbone, making another shudder rack her body.

"You do not find our kisses pleasurable?"

She closed her eyes as she battled the dizzying need that clutched deep within her.

"Too pleasurable. I can not think when you hold me like this."

"Then do not think. Just enjoy," he commanded, returning his lips to her mouth with a barely restrained hunger.

Rachel melted against him, her hands stroking the firm muscles of his chest. For the moment it did not matter what magic he possessed that set her body ablaze. She only knew that she wished to discover where these tumultuous sensations would lead.

Then without warning Anthony was pulling away and glancing toward the shadowed garden.

"What is it?" she whispered, feeling oddly bereft as his hands dropped to his side.

"I heard something," he retorted, moving toward the stone railing.

Rachel followed him, her own gaze probing the

darkness until she at last spotted the vague outline of two forms beside a distant fountain.

"Someone is in the garden," she whispered, pointing toward the figures. "Over there."

He leaned forward, his gaze narrowed. "It appears to be your uncle."

Rachel felt a stab of unease as she recognized the unmistakable shape of her father and the smaller, obviously female form with him.

"Yes," she breathed, instinctively moving toward the nearby stairs, "and Miss Carlfield."

She had taken only a few steps before Anthony had reached out to grasp her arm in a restraining grip.

"Where are you going?"

She glanced at him in surprise. "To speak with them."

"I do not believe they wish to be interrupted."

"They should not be out here alone."

He smiled wryly at her impatient words. "Neither s—should we, my dear."

The truth of his words sent a warm heat to her countenance. Still, it did not lessen her unease.

"What if Mr. Carlfield or Mr. Wingrove should happen out here and catch them?" she demanded.

"It is their risk to take, Rachel," he said with firm insistence. "We should not interfere."

She heaved a sigh, giving a reluctant shake of her head. He was right, of course. Although her father could be wildly impulsive and anxious to take risks that would make most gentlemen tremble in fear, he was a grown man capable of choosing his own path. It was not her place to chastise him for his behavior. Especially not when her body still throbbed from Anthony's bold caresses.

"You are always so logical," she murmured.

He gave a short laugh. "No, not always, I fear."

She met his wry gaze. "No?"

"If I were l—logical I would pack my bags and leave for London before I am completely under your spell."

Her heart came to a halt at the thought of him disappearing from her life.

"But you will not?" she demanded.

"No." His hand lifted to gently cup her cheek. "Like a moth I will dance close to the flame. I can not seem to resist."

Nine

Broswell Park was a ponderous house built of heavy gray stones with two long wings awkwardly attached to the main building. Behind the imposing structure was a tidy garden that was laid out in a predictable manner with the proper beddings and occasional fountains scattered near the pathways.

Like a queen presiding over her court, Lady Broswell was situated near the long tables groaning beneath a vast array of food and numerous bottles of champagne. About her the guests mingled and chatted with seeming indifference to the fact that they had seen each other every evening for the past fortnight.

Rachel stood with her father at the edge of the garden, watching the elegant scene with a jaundiced gaze. Although she had been anxious to see the home of her aunt and cousins, she discovered that it was as cold and impersonal as the people who inhabited it.

"Well, what do you think, my dearest?" her father murmured.

"It is precisely as I expected," she retorted with a grimace. "Solid, respectable and utterly boring."

The green eyes flashed with amusement. "Lady

Broswell has never been accused of possessing an imagination."

"No, she is determinedly tedious." Her gaze lingered on Lady Broswell's aloof expression and stiff form encased in a heavy gray gown. "Still, it is rather depressing."

"The view?"

She waved a hand to include the entire garden. "Everything. The house, the gardens, and even the Misses Hamlin. It is all quite perfect, but there is no life behind the proper image. It is as if one were regarding a well-arranged painting upon a wall."

The Devilish Dandy gave a slow nod of agreement. "You are quite right, of course. Lady Broswell has always considered her image of prime importance. Absurd notions of warmth and kindness and even love are meaningless when compared to the need to present an appearance of lofty superiority."

A pang tugged at Rachel's heart at the sheer waste of it all. Lady Broswell was a lady of means and position. She could have whatever she wished and yet she had chosen a shallow existence that benefited no one.

"Do you suppose it makes her happy?"

Solomon gave a shake of his head. "No, but it satisfies her pride."

She turned to meet her father's gaze. "I would rather be happy."

His expression softened as he regarded her upturned countenance.

"That is what I wish for you. This is nothing more than an empty setting without love and a family."

"Yes."

"I am very pleased that both Sarah and Emma have found such happiness."

Rachel smiled as she thought of her sisters. She

missed their companionship, but she knew they were well satisfied with their choice of prospective husbands. And who could blame them? Although Lord Chance could be a trifle arrogant, he was well matched with the strong-willed Sarah and no one who met Lord Hartshore could deny that he was thoroughly besotted with the gentle Emma.

"As am I."

A speculative expression descended upon the lean countenance. "Now I have only to see you suitably settled and I shall have done my duty."

Rachel waved a chiding finger in his direction. "Do not turn your matchmaking efforts upon me, Father," she warned. "I have no interest in being under the heel of any gentleman."

"Fah. Do you believe either Sarah or Emma are under the heels of their fiancés?"

The very fact that she had lately begun to wonder if being at the mercy of one gentleman in particular would be so terribly bad made her determinedly square her shoulders. She was not a maiden destined to become a traditional wife and mother. It was ludicrous to even think of such things.

Ludicrous, and somehow vaguely painful.

"They are fortunate in their choices," she said in firm tones.

"I have no doubt that you will be equally fortunate." A rather mysterious smile curved his lips. "Of course, a gentleman would have to possess great courage and fortitude to willingly acquire you as a bride."

A dangerous spark entered the hazel eyes at his deliberate teasing.

"Indeed?"

"You can not deny that you are extraordinarily stubborn and far too fond of having your own way," he said dryly. "You have also been shamelessly spoiled by your numerous admirers."

"I must wonder if I shall ever discover a gentleman who would wish such a shrew," she mocked.

He shrugged in a negligent manner. "Oh, I believe we shall be able to hunt down one gentleman who possesses the necessary pluck to dare the challenge."

Rachel rolled her eyes. "You relieve me greatly."

The Devilish Dandy gave a bark of laughter, his expression fond as he reached out to tap the end of her slender nose.

"Ah, Rachel, you are indeed a rare and independent creature, but your heart will demand that you seek someone to love. Like your sisters you will need a gentleman who is true and honorable and strong enough to tame your wild tendencies."

She shifted uneasily as the sudden image of Anthony's countenance rose to mind. She did not doubt that he was true and honorable. And certainly he had a habit of making her want to behave in a manner that would make him proud of her.

But her father was wrong. She was not like her sisters. Instead she was far more in the image of the Devilish Dandy.

"At the moment I have no desire to be tamed," she quipped lightly.

He smiled in a complacent fashion. "I sense that you will soon alter your opinion."

Rachel was not at all certain that she liked the confident assurance in his tone.

"And what makes you say such an absurd thing?"

Rather than replying, the Devilish Dandy raised his quizzing glass to regard the paunchy gentleman bearing down upon them attired in a hideous puce coat.

"Egads, we are about to be descended upon." The Devilish Dandy gave a delicate shudder. "Would you just look at that atrocity of a coat? It is really bad enough to be forced to endure the man's coarse manners and lack of wit. To also be constantly insulted by his glaring want for taste is really more than any gentleman should be forced to bear."

Although rather relieved to have the unsettling conversation brought to an end, Rachel regarded Mr. Carlfield with barely hidden dislike.

Her time under his roof had not improved her initial impression of the gentleman.

Quite frankly he was a buffoon.

Not only for his callous determination to marry off his daughter to save his worthless hide, but for his supreme lack of anything approaching intelligence. Heavens, he actually boasted that he had never finished reading a book and that a true gentleman never bothered thinking about anything beyond a rousing card game and his current mistress.

How Violet could be even remotely related to the fool went beyond all imagination.

"Mr. Foxworth," Mr. Carlfield puffed, rubbing his hands together in a manner that set Rachel's teeth on edge. "A lovely party, is it not?"

The Devilish Dandy dropped his quizzing glass with a languid motion.

"Tedious, I should say."

"Oh, well, country gatherings are rather dull when compared to London," Mr. Carlfield readily agreed, anxious to appear a gentleman of sophistication. "Lady Broswell does offer a fine spread, however. Her chef is French, you know."

Solomon waved a dismissive hand at the proud claim. "Any fool with a cleaver and a ludicrous accent can pass himself as a chef. A true artist has no need to disguise his inadequacies in heavy sauces."

"Oh yes, quite true." The older gentleman paused

before loudly clearing his throat. "Ah, I have some gentlemen who are quite anxious to meet you, Mr. Foxworth."

"I thought you might," the Devilish Dandy drawled in bored tones. "I do hope they are not related to Mr. Wingrove. My constitution could not bear the grim stupidity."

Rachel was forced to duck her head as she smothered a giggle. Mr. Carlfield, however, obviously did not realize that he was being mocked by the elegant gentleman.

"No, no. Fine chaps, I assure you. Quite up to the mark."

"I fear I do not believe in miracles." Solomon heaved a sigh as he turned his attention to Rachel. "Well, my dear, it appears that I must leave you to your own devises for a time. Do try not to break too many hearts while I am gone."

She raised her sparkling eyes and quirked her brow. "I shall be on my very best behavior."

"That is what worries me," he murmured before allowing himself to be led away by the anxious Mr. Carlfield.

Rachel chuckled, knowing her father fully intended to enjoy his role as the caustic, wretchedly arrogant Mr. Foxworth. She might have felt pity for the other gentlemen if they weren't so deserving of a good set-down.

Once alone, Rachel glanced toward Lady Broswell. She knew that it would be a perfect opportunity to rile the older woman's temper. What could be more galling than having Rachel at her home with no means of retaliation? But on the drive over Rachel had already determined what she intended to accomplish this afternoon. For the moment it was more important than her plot for revenge.

Glancing about to make sure that she was not being watched, Rachel slowly strolled along a low hedge until she was certain she was out of sight of the guests. Only then did she seek out a method of slipping into the house.

At last finding a doorway, she stepped into a long hall with an open-beamed ceiling. Not surprisingly it was as depressingly formal as the garden, with heavy shields on the paneled walls and suits of armor standing at rigid attention. Making her way through the heavy shadows, she at last discovered what she was looking for.

A heavy-set woman with a bundle of keys attached to her somber gown, proclaiming her to be the housekeeper.

Rachel had already discovered that the woman had been a servant at Broswell Park for the past twenty years. Certainly long enough to know the truth of poor Julia hidden in the dowager house.

Busily arranging a bowl of freshly cut flowers, the woman did not notice Rachel's approach until she was nearly upon her. With a start of surprise she abruptly turned to regard the sudden intruder.

"Oh."

Rachel smiled in a charming fashion. "Forgive me. I did not intend to startle you."

Swiftly recovering, the servant ran her hands over her apron. "May I help you?"

"Thank you, but I merely wish for a place to rest from the sun for a moment."

"Of course." With brisk motions a chair was pulled from further down the hall and Rachel was urged to settle on the brocade cushion. Once assured she was comfortable, the woman gave a nod of her head. "I shall leave you to your rest."

"A moment, please." Rachel hastily halted her departure.

With a faint start of surprise the servant obediently halted. "Yes?"

Rachel paused, knowing that she would have to be extremely careful not to arouse undue suspicion. She did not make the mistake of most aristocrats in assuming that servants were stupid or incapable of understanding what was happening about them. She knew that there was little in the household that was not fully discussed below stairs.

"Are you the housekeeper?"

"Yes. I am Mrs. Stalton."

"Have you been with Lady Broswell long?"

"Near on twenty years."

"Ah." She smiled again, hoping Mrs. Stalton would dismiss her chatter as that of a rather dimwitted maiden. "This is a lovely house. You must be very proud."

The compliment had the desired effective of lessening the natural restraint of the older woman.

"I do my best."

"That is obvious. Not that I am surprised. My mother often said that Lady Broswell was most particular."

A grimace was barely suppressed at the mention of the overbearing matron.

"That she is. Your mother was acquainted with Lady Broswell?"

"Yes, although it has been several years since they have seen one another." Rachel deliberately paused, her head tilting to one side. "You know, it is the oddest thing."

"What is?"

"I was certain that my mother said that Lady

Broswell possessed three daughters, and yet, there are only two."

A sharp silence fell as the housekeeper nervously clutched her hands together.

"Yes, well, the youngest died when she was just a babe."

Rachel felt a fierce flare of satisfaction. So, her suspicions were correct. There had been a third daughter. Although she would bet her last quid that she had not died as a babe.

"Oh, how horrid," she forced herself to murmur in sympathy. "I did not know."

"It was a terribly tragedy," Mrs. Stalton said stiffly.

"I believe her name was Julia, was it not?"

Obviously disturbed, the housekeeper glanced over her shoulder as if she feared Lady Broswell might suddenly emerge from the shadows.

"I believe so. Now, you must excuse me. I am very busy today."

This time Rachel did not attempt to halt the housekeeper as she scurried away. Indeed, she doubted that a team of oxen could halt her determined flight. Besides, she had already discovered the truth she had been seeking.

Julia was indeed the daughter of Lady Broswell. And the woman had deliberately hidden her away from the world, pretending that she had died.

Rising to her feet, Rachel slowly made her way back to the garden.

She realized that she had discovered the answers she had desired, but she hadn't the least notion what she intended to do with the information.

She was still pondering the dilemma as she entered the garden and made her way back along the hedge. Lost in her thoughts, she did not notice the slender gentleman hurrying in her direction until too late.

"Miss Cresswell, there you are." Reaching her side, Lord Newell smiled in relief. "I feared that you had left."

Rachel bit back a curse of annoyance. She was in no mood to play the role of flirt. She simply wished to be on her own so that she could consider what she had learned.

"Good afternoon, my lord," she said, her expression impatient.

"Please, can you not call me George?"

She ignored his soft plea, wanting only to be rid of his persistent attentions.

"Should you not be with Miss Hamlin?"

He gave a deliberate shudder. "I do not wish to ruin such a beautiful afternoon with talk of Miss Hamlin. I would much rather discuss you."

"A rather tedious subject, I would think."

"Tedious?" He stepped closer, nearly overwhelming her with the heavy scent of his cologne. "How could one tire of speaking of your beauty or the charm of your smile?"

Her lips thinned. "How, indeed?"

"Would you care to walk beside the lake?" he asked eagerly. "Or perhaps we could enjoy the shade of the grotto?"

Not about to be alone with this man so that he could clumsily grope at her, Rachel gave a firm shake of her head.

"I do not believe that would be wise."

"I do not wish to be wise. I only want to be alone with you," he said with a petulant frown.

"I think it best that you return to the others."

"But why?" he demanded. "Have I offended you?"

Gads, what would it take to rid herself of this man?

"Of course not."

"Then why are you avoiding me?"

"I merely have no desire to create undue gossip."

"You have never concerned yourself with gossip before."

"My concern is for you," Rachel said, suddenly struck by inspiration. There was one certain means of driving Lord Newell from her vicinity. "My uncle can be swift to anger and even more swift to use his dueling pistols to soothe his pride."

The boyish countenance abruptly drained of color at her casual threat.

"Good Lord."

"I think it best that we take care until we return to London."

He gave a furtive glance toward the Devilish Dandy, obviously not relishing the thought of a duel at dawn. Even if she were an angel fallen from heaven.

"Yes, perhaps you are right. I shall call upon you when we return to town."

She flashed him a smile. "A most sensible notion."

Anthony had no intention of attending the garden party. He had no desire to witness Rachel continuing her determined game of revenge. He found it oddly disturbing. Not that he feared she possessed a truly spiteful nature. Her love for her family and kindness toward Julia was proof of her tender heart. But there was something deeper beneath her open dislike of Lady Broswell. Something he could not put his finger on.

Besides, he had told himself, he still had a few last-minute touches to finish with his current invention.

But after an hour in the stables he had reluctantly acknowledged that he could not stay away.

Rachel was youthful and passionate enough to plunge herself into disaster. And Anthony had little faith that her unpredictable uncle could hope to restrain her. It was clearly his responsibility see to it that she did not become too outrageous.

Convincing himself that his urgency to be at Rachel's side was more a matter of duty than a mere aching desire to see her smile, he had hurriedly bathed and changed. Then, deciding it would be quicker to walk than call for his carriage, he had cut through the nearby woods and angled across the parkland to arrive directly in the gardens.

He had just reached the hedge when he heard the sound of Rachel's voice, clearly followed by the pleas of Lord Newell.

At first Anthony was forced to exercise undue restraint to keep from plunging through the hedge and blackening the forward fool's eye. Absurd, considering he had never experienced a twinge of jealousy in his life. But even as his hands clenched at his side he heard Rachel firmly threatening the boy with visions of dueling her uncle.

His annoyance had fled to be replaced with undeniable surprise. Hearing Lord Newell scurry away, he stepped around the hedge to confront the woman who was a constant plague to his thoughts.

"Well, I must admit to being rather bewildered, my dove," he said in low tones.

Her eyes widened at his sudden appearance, appearing quite fetching in a brilliant sapphire gown and straw hat with matching ribbons.

"Anthony, I did not think you would be here," she said, not bothering to disguise her pleasure at his sudden appearance.

Anthony's heart warmed and any unease at the knowledge he was not nearly so comfortable alone with his work as he used to be was dismissed.

"I became bored with my own company. I thought I w—would amuse myself by watching you vex Lady Broswell. It appears that my trip was in vain, however."

Her expression became guarded at his words. "I do not know what you mean."

"Oh, come, Rachel, you have obviously lured young Newell into your web for the sole purpose of making Lady Broswell gnash her teeth."

"Perhaps I simply find him charming."

Anthony stepped forward, clasping her chin in a firm grip. "N—no, he is far too weak and easily swayed to tempt you."

The hazel eyes sparkled in a deliberate challenge. "Surely a lady of sense would prefer a gentleman who is malleable? Far more comfortable than a gentleman who refuses to do as one wishes."

His gaze swept over her pale features, lingering on the stubborn line of her jaw.

"You would be bored witless in an hour. Only a challenge would suit your passionate nature."

"You are very confident that you know me."

"Not nearly as well as I would desire to know you." Her eyes abruptly darkened at his soft words and Anthony felt a fierce stab of need. He remembered the evening two nights ago when he had held her and caressed her with such intimacy. Good heavens, he had never wanted a woman as desperately as he wanted this one. "By God, you could tempt a saint. And I have n—never been a saint."

She swayed forward, then seeming to abruptly remember that they were in full sight of the other guests, she took a hasty step backward.

"I should return to my uncle."

"In a moment." He halted her retreat. "First I wish to know why you chose to send that eager whelp back to Lady Broswell rather than further your revenge."

She gave a shrug. "Does it matter?"

"Yes, I rather think that it does."

She paused for a long moment before giving a restless shake of her head.

"In truth I am not certain," she grudgingly admitted. "I merely was in no humor to endure his tedious company."

Anthony smiled with gentle understanding. "Perhaps you are beginning to realize that revenge is a hollow triumph."

Not surprisingly, she promptly shied away from the hint that her determination might be weakening.

"More likely I ate something that did not agree with me," she said tartly. "Shall we join the others?"

Anthony chuckled in appreciation at her undeniable spirit as he firmly placed her hand upon his arm.

"By all means, my dear. We shall retrieve some champagne to settle that sour stomach of yours."

Ten

The morning had dawned with a dismal promise of rain. Heavy gray clouds hung low in the skies, making most guests linger in their beds and sip their hot chocolate rather than brave the chilled rooms downstairs.

Anthony, however, ignored the impending rain and attiring himself in his black coat and breeches, he made his way downstairs to partake of a generous breakfast. Once finished, he left a brief note that he commanded to be delivered to Miss Cresswell after luncheon and headed for the stables.

Nearly three hours later he was at last satisfied that his project was perfected. Saddling his horse, he made his way to the distant dowager house, a smile touching his mouth as the clouds began to flee and the sun made a welcome appearance.

It promised to be a glorious afternoon, he acknowledged. Perfect for his plans.

He managed to slip Julia from the house with his usual ease, pushing her chair out of the fenced yard to the meadow beyond. Once there, he calmly settled her on the gentle mare he had brought with him to the house and carefully strapped her into the saddle he had devoted the past fortnight to constructing.

It was ingenious in design. The high back supported her spine while a number of padded straps were attached to the saddle along with buckles so that Julia would be firmly locked into place.

It took some time for him to satisfy himself that there would be no danger to the young girl. Without the use of her legs it would be entirely the saddle's responsibility to hold her upright and in place.

His careful inspection was accompanied by ceaseless chatter from Julia, who was utterly delighted by his surprise. Glancing at her animated countenance, he realized that she was a far different child from the one he and Rachel had discovered sitting listlessly beside the window.

That young girl had been resigned to her life of bored loneliness. There had been no hope, no spark within those pale blue eyes. Now they shimmered with an undeniable excitement.

A faint pang of unease entered his heart at the knowledge that both he and Rachel had unwittingly made a mark on Julia's life. Her placid world had been temporarily disturbed and she had tasted the world about her. What would happen when they left and she was once again on her own?

He abruptly shoved the question aside to be brooded upon later. Today he intended to see to it at least one of her dreams came true.

"I believe we are prepared," he at last announced as he straightened. "Now we have only to wait for Miss Cresswell to arrive."

"I can not wait for her to see me," Julia breathed.

Anthony heard the faint click of the front gate and he flashed his anxious companion a reassuring smile.

"I do not believe you will have to wait long."

"How surprised she will be to see me."

"Surprised, indeed," he agreed, glancing over the

buckles once again to reassure himself they were tight. "You are certain that you are quite secure?"

She gave a small wiggle. "I could not fall if I attempted to do so."

"And you will remember to hang on tightly?"

"Do you always fuss so?" she demanded with a laugh.

He offered a rueful smile. "Yes, I f—fear that I do. One must take care when one is preparing to fly."

"I will hold tightly," she promised with a twinkle in her eyes.

"Good."

Knowing that she was indeed safe, Anthony took the reins of the mare firmly in hand before pulling himself onto his own mount.

In a conspiratory silence they listened to Rachel cross the yard. He had specifically requested that she meet him behind the dowager house in the note that he had left. He hadn't, however, revealed the surprise awaiting her.

"Hello?" Rachel at last called out in puzzlement. "Julia?"

"She is here," Anthony retorted with a glance toward his companion.

"I am ready," Julia whispered in answer to his silent question.

From behind the trees that hid them from view, Anthony watched Rachel push open the back gate and enter the small meadow. She glanced about in obvious bewilderment and Anthony gave a firm nod to the waiting Julia.

"Here we go."

Urging his mount into a canter, Anthony pulled the mare behind him, keeping careful watch on the girl, who was grinning with obvious delight. Together they circled the meadow nearly a dozen times, Julia's laughter ringing through the air. The blond hair tumbled about her flushed countenance, making her appear as young and carefree as a child.

"Look, Miss Cresswell, I am flying," Julia called in pure happiness.

"You most certainly are," Rachel readily applauded. "It is wonderful."

"Faster, Mr. Clarke," the girl urged.

With an indulgent smile Anthony increased the pace for one more turn about the meadow before bringing the horses to a halt beside the gate. Vaulting to the ground he moved to undo the numerous buckles.

"I believe that is enough for now," he said in firm tones. "I would not wish you to become stiff."

"Very well," she agreed with a faint sigh.

In moments he had her free and was lifting her down to carefully place her in the bath chair and covering her with a blanket.

"Well, it appears, my dear, that you have fulfilled one of your wishes," Rachel said as she gently brushed a strand of blond hair behind the girl's ear.

"It was most wonderful," Julia breathed. "I felt as though I were indeed flying."

Rachel abruptly lifted her head to regard Anthony with a warm smile. A smile that Anthony felt to the very tips of his toes.

"It was very clever of Mr. Clarke," she said softly.

"I am glad you approve," he murmured with a dip of his head.

"And very kind," she concluded.

"Oh yes," Julia promptly agreed.

Anthony gave a chuckle. "Enough. You shall quite put me to the blush."

Julia reached out to grasp his hand. "But I do not know how I can ever thank you."

"No thanks are necessary between friends." He gave her fingers a slight squeeze. "And we are friends, are w—we not?"

"I should like to think so," she said wistfully.

Freeing his hand, Anthony reached into his pocket to retrieve the small horse he had carved from a piece of mahogany. Although it was no masterpiece it was delicately detailed with a pair of dainty wings set on the back.

"Here. I made this so you could always remember the day you flew."

With reverent care the maiden took the horse from his hands, running a finger over the polished wood.

"Oh, it is beautiful. Do you see, Miss Cresswell? It has wings."

"It is perfect." Rachel obligingly admired the carving. "Quite perfect."

Julia lifted the horse to press it to her cheek, then without warning she promptly burst into tears.

Caught off guard, Anthony bent beside the chair.

"Here, here. I meant for you to smile, not drown yourself in tears."

Julia managed a watery smile. "It is just that I have never had a real friend before. I believe it is just as wonderful as flying."

"Yes, I do believe you are right," he said gently. "Now, as much as I regret ending our afternoon I fear it is time to return you to the house."

The glow in the blue eyes dimmed at his regretful words.

"So soon?"

Anthony disliked the thought of her returning to the dark house as much as the young girl. But he was sensible enough to realize they had courted enough danger for the moment.

"We do not wish to be caught. It would be an end to our afternoons together."

"I suppose."

"We shall see you soon, my dear," Rachel promised as Anthony moved to the back of the chair.

"I am glad that you came to see me fly."

Rachel smiled. "As am I."

"I will return in a moment," Anthony said to Rachel as he pushed the chair back through the gate and toward the house.

It took a few moments to settle Julia beside the window, her new wooden horse hidden in a small drawer, before he was able to return to Rachel.

He discovered her waiting for him patiently beside the horses, and collecting the reins, he indicated that he was ready to leave.

They skirted the wall about the dowager property, heading toward the nearby woods. Feeling Rachel's gaze upon him, Anthony turned his head to meet her quizzical regard.

"Yes?"

She slowly smiled. "You are an amazing gentleman, Mr. Clarke."

"Hardly amazing, my dear."

"But you are," she protested. "I know of no other gentleman who would have given a second thought to Julia, let alone devote so much time to granting her wish."

His smile became rueful as he thought of the vulnerable child. "Well, I have a peculiar s—sympathy for those less than perfect."

The hazel eyes darkened with an indefinable emotion. "I happen to think you are quite perfect, Mr.

Clarke, and I would thank you to halt your persistence in believing otherwise."

His breath caught at her fierce words, a magical sense of wonderment flowering in his heart. Suddenly he realized that when he was with Rachel he did feel perfect. Gloriously perfect with no need to remain in the shadows or disappear into his workroom.

"Would you, indeed?"

"Yes."

He allowed his gaze to lower to the full promise of her lips. "And I happen to think you are the most bewitching creature it has ever been my pleasure to encounter."

Those lips parted in the most enticing manner, but even as he considered the logistics of maintaining control of the horses while thoroughly kissing this adorable minx, there was the distinct sound of footsteps running deeper into the woods.

Rachel came to a startled halt, her eyes wide. "Anthony?"

"I heard," he said quietly, pressing the reins into her hands. Moving forward, he peered through the heavy underbrush, unable to catch more than a brief glimpse of a fleeing form. "Damn."

"Do you see anyone?" Rachel called.

"They have disappeared."

About to return to Rachel, he was suddenly distracted by a glint of gold upon the ground. Bending down, he scooped the small button from the dirt.

"What is it?" Rachel demanded as she moved to join him.

Anthony studied the object in the dappled light. "A button from a uniform, I believe."

"Heavens, what odd objects we seem to find in these woods. First a brooch and now a button. Perhaps this place is haunted."

Anthony could envision a far more prosaic reason for the woods to be littered with bits and pieces of clothing. He flashed her a wicked grin.

"I w—would guess that the specters haunting these woods have not yet seen the inside of a grave."

She was swift to follow the direction of his thoughts and her golden brows lifted.

"A lovers' tryst?"

"Yes."

She glanced around the thick line of trees, then noted the underbrush that would offer protection from the hard ground.

"It is rather a romantic location, you must admit."

Anthony gritted his teeth as a predictable heat surged through his body. A heat that was becoming more and more difficult to contain.

"Good gads, do not put such dangerous thoughts in my mind."

Her expression became coy as she fluttered the ridiculously long lashes. "Do you mean to tell me they were not already there?"

Anthony gave a bark of laughter. He never felt so alive as he did with this woman.

"Minx," he chided, taking the reins from her hands. "Let us go while I am able to maintain a thread of common sense."

He firmly led them from the tempting isolation of the trees, for once aware that his legendary self-control was in dire danger of going up in flames. Rachel readily followed his lead, although there was a decidedly pleased smile on her lips.

Clearly she enjoyed the sensation of rattling his composure, he wryly acknowledged.

They crossed the parkland and as they entered the courtyard Anthony lifted a hand toward a young groom. The servant hurried forward to offer a swift bow.

"Sir."

"Take the horses to the stables." He held out the reins to the lad.

"At once."

With an odd glance at the unusual saddle on the mare, the servant hurried away, leaving Anthony free to concentrate on the maiden at his side.

Turning, he met her teasing glance.

"Are you not about to disappear, sir?" she asked in light tones.

He raised his brows. "Not unless you wish me to, my dear."

"Of course not." Her swift denial stirred a glow of satisfaction within him until she managed to dampen his smug pleasure with her artless smile. "Indeed, I particularly have something that I wish to show you."

His smile was wry as he gave a faint nod of his head. So much for his irresistible charm.

"I am at your disposal."

With a mysterious smile she headed straight for the house. Anthony readily followed, amused by her obvious anticipation.

There was a vivid energy about her that was utterly captivating. This woman would never be content to live her life in the quiet, placid style that was expected by society. She would charge boldly through the world with no concern that she was not nearly as comfortably predictable as most gentlemen preferred.

They entered the house through a side door and leading him to a narrow staircase used by the servants, she began climbing to the third floor.

Reaching the landing, she swept past the large ball-room and at last halted in a small, dark alcove.

Coming to stand close enough to inhale the sweet scent of roses, he regarded her shadowed countenance.

"Why, Rachel, are you once again leading me to some remote spot to have your evil way with me? You must think of my r—reputation."

She cast him a dry glance. "Do you see this?"

He followed the direction of her outstretched hand. "It looks remarkably like a common door. Hardly an astonishing discover."

"That is because you do not yet know what lies beyond it." She reached her hand into the reticule she carried to withdraw a small key. Bending forward she inserted it into the lock.

"Where did you get that?" he demanded in surprise.

"My maid was kind enough to borrow it from the housekeeper."

"Borrow or steal?" he demanded.

"Well, I could not risk unwelcome questions," she retorted, pushing the door open and dropping the key back into her reticule.

Without hesitation she plunged through the doorway and began climbing the short flight of stairs directly behind the door. Not nearly as eager, Anthony followed behind, plucking at the numerous cobwebs that threatened to cling to his coat.

"Gads, I do not believe anyone has been through here in the past century."

"We must be quiet," she warned as she stepped into the room atop the stairs.

Waiting until he had joined her, she pushed aside a heavy curtain opposite the stairs to reveal a vast room below them. With a faint prick of surprise Anthony realized that they were standing on a narrow balcony.

"The ballroom," he said softly, noting the servant across the room scrubbing the floor. He glanced around the balcony, a frown marring his wide brow. "Surely this is much too small for the orchestra?"

"My maid discovered that it was built for visiting royalty to enjoy the various balls."

That explained the gruesomely ornate chairs beside the railing, he acknowledged with a grimace.

"And did a large number of Royals visit Carlfield Manor?"

She gave a low chuckle as she absently brushed at the dust clinging to her pretty buttercup silk gown.

"No, but the mere fact that you possess a Royal Box makes one appear far more superior."

Anthony gave a shake of his head at the faded gilding and threadbare velvet curtains.

"I do not believe Prinny would be especially pleased to discover the sadly neglected state of his box. Still, I am not quite certain what your interest in this moldy location is."

She regarded him as if surprised by his thorough lack of perception. "Do you not see? It is perfect."

"I must apologize for my slow wits," he said with gentle mockery, "but I fear I do not see at all. What is it perfect for, beyond ruining the shine upon my boots?"

"To hide Julia, of course," she said impatiently. "So that she can attend her first ball."

Anthony did not attempt to hide his shock at her feather-brained scheme.

"Good God."

Oblivious to his patent lack of enthusiasm to her plot, she regarded him with a sparkling gaze.

"She has already informed me that Mrs. Greene

puts her to bed shortly after nine and then returns upstairs to enjoy her dinner in her own chambers. She does not return to check on her until the next morning unless Julia rings the bell."

He supposed that he should not be surprised at her audacious plot. She thought nothing of shocking society or flaunting her intimate connection with the Devilish Dandy. Why would she not suggest kidnapping a girl from the safety of her bed and smuggling her into a house crammed to the rafters so she could enjoy her first ball?

Still, he found himself wanting to hear about the madcap scheme from her own lips.

"Are you suggesting that we steal Julia from her bed and sneak her into this balcony?"

"Yes." She smiled with unnerving confidence, making Anthony's heart sink. There was a stubborn set to that lovely jaw that he did not like at all. "We will pull the curtains until there is only a small space for her to see through. She will attend the ball and wear her new gown just as she wished."

Anthony narrowed his gaze. "And how do your propose that we achieve this amazing feat?"

She regarded him in a superior fashion. "I have all the details worked out."

Anthony rolled his eyes, knowing he was lost.

"Heaven help me."

Eleven

Rachel had been singularly unprepared for the vast effort that it required to play the role of fairy godmother.

On the surface her plan to let Julia attend the ball had seemed simple enough. It was only when Anthony had demanded concise details that she realized just how difficult it would be to accomplish her goal.

The balcony had to be thoroughly cleaned without attracting the attentions of the servants or guests, the ball gown had to be retrieved from the dressmaker and smuggled to Julia, then Rachel was forced to dress for the ball several hours early so that her maid could go with Anthony to prepare the girl for her special evening. He was to bring her to Carlfield Manor in his carriage and carry her up the servants' staircase to the balcony.

It was exhausting and at times nerve-wracking, but at last Rachel had nothing left to do but leave her room and join the seemingly endless guests that crowded the ballroom.

As she had intended, her appearance created a decided rustle in the room. Unlike the other maidens, she was attired in a deep-ruby gown that precisely matched the jewel about her neck. White crepe roses studded with rubies encircled the hem and formed a wreath in her golden curls. The neckline was low-cut with tiny puff sleeves that exposed a great deal of snowy-white skin.

It was a daring, vibrant gown that she had chosen to bring a furious frown to Lady Broswell's ugly countenance. Rachel, however, did not even glance over to where her aunt glowered and stewed beside her insipid daughters. Instead she busily began to dismiss the eager admirers that crowded about her so that she could keep a covert watch on the balcony across from her.

Despite her confident determination to ensure that Julia was allowed to enjoy the ball, she was not impervious to the risk they were taking.

Anything might go astray.

Mrs. Greene might discover Julia missing and raise the alarm.

Anthony might be seen carrying Julia to the stairs at the end of the corridor.

Julia might become overexcited and reveal her position on the balcony.

Or a curious servant might decide to creep into the little-used balcony to gaze upon the guests and discover the hidden maiden.

Rachel was all-too aware that it was no doubt poor Julia who would suffer the consequences of discovery. She could only pray that all went smoothly and that the child felt the excitement of her first ball was worth the danger they courted.

Having at last rid herself of even the most persistent suitor, Rachel absently sipped her champagne and pretended to enjoy the couples beginning to twirl about the dance floor. Instead her gaze was darting toward the curtains surrounding the balcony. At least Julia would have an excellent view of the dancers, she acknowledged. The four large chandeliers blazed with enough candles to flood the entire room with flickering light.

She thought that she had just noted a tiny ripple in one of the curtains when she suddenly was interrupted by the sight of Violet pressing her way through the crowd toward her.

As was appropriate, the young lady was attired in a white gown with a modest neckline. A profusion of pink ribbons dotted the hem and large puffed sleeves. Unfortunately the color and style did nothing to enhance her pale features and rounded curves.

Not that the most skilled seamstress could have created the image of a glittering prospective bride, Rachel thought with a pang. There was a deep, unshakable misery in those dark eyes that sent a flare of concern through Rachel.

Coming to a halt beside her, Violet regarded her with a trace of envy.

"Oh, Rachel, how very beautiful you are."

Rachel smiled gently. "Thank you, Violet. And you, of course, look lovely."

Violet grimaced, clearly as aware as Rachel of the limitations of her gown.

"That is very kind, but I always look wretchedly insipid in white. How I wish I possessed your courage to wear what I desire."

"That is one of the privileges of being born into scandal," Rachel said in wry tones. "The old tabbies are bound to gossip about me regardless of what I do, so I might as well give them something outrageous to discuss."

Violet appeared to consider her words, her hands absently opening and shutting her ivory fan.

"Does the scandal bother you overly much?"

Rachel was surprised by the question. Even though they were friends, Violet had always taken excruciating care to avoid any mention of Rachel's sordid connection to the Devilish Dandy, or even her own habit of setting tongues wagging.

"Not at all," she retorted with blunt honesty. "Those who are my true friends seek beyond the gossip. The others do not concern me."

Violet gnawed her bottom lip until Rachel feared she might draw blood.

"What of those who give you the cut direct?"

Rachel shrugged. "Few dare."

"Yes, that is true enough," her companion murmured.

Rachel narrowed her gaze as her initial concern became threaded with a growing sense of unease. Why the devil was Violet suddenly so interested in a life of scandal? Surely this sweet, biddable child was not considering anything drastic? The mere thought was enough to freeze her heart.

"Is something wrong?" she asked softly.

Violet's gaze abruptly dropped to her fan, which was rapidly becoming frayed beyond repair.

"I was merely thinking that scandal has not interfered in your life. Indeed, you have been very happy with the freedom to do as you choose."

Her words only deepened Rachel's unease to downright fear. Gads, had she possibly said anything to urge Violet into an act she might very well regret the rest of her life?

"Violet, are you considering doing something scandalous?" she asked in cautious tones.

"Me?" Violet gave a forced laugh. "I am not nearly so daring as you."

Far from convinced, Rachel reached out to grasp her friend's hand, her expression uncommonly somber. Although the scandal in her own life had never been particularly bothersome, she had seen how it had wounded her sensitive sister, Emma, and to a lesser extent even Sarah. She would not wish to allow Violet to be carried away with some romantic notion that scandal did not require its own peculiar price.

"My dearest, I will admit that I do not wish to see you married to Mr. Wingrove, but there is no need to do anything hasty. If you wish to come with me to London so you can consider your future, you have only to tell me."

The youthful features became shuttered, as if Violet abruptly regretted speaking at all.

"Yes, thank you."

"Violet."

"Forgive me, I must join Father."

Before Rachel could protest, Violet had pulled free of her grasp and began pushing her way back through the thick crowd.

Rachel resisted the urge to charge after her. The middle of a ballroom was hardly the place to coerce a confession from her friend. Even supposing Violet would be willing to confess what she was plotting.

Besides, she reminded herself sternly, she had quite enough to worry about this evening as it was.

Unconsciously tapping her foot, Rachel anxiously scanned the passing guests in search of the familiar handsome countenance.

Several long moments passed until she at last caught a glimpse of Anthony's lean form weaving its way in her direction. A deep surge of relief rushed through her at the same moment her heart flopped at the sight of him attired in pure black silk with only his crisp white cravat and silk shirt to provide relief.

She had been correct when she had first caught sight of him at the opera house, she mused with a delicious furl of excitement. He did possess a fine pair of shoulders. And broad chest. And firm legs. And . . . she shivered, determinedly returning her thoughts to the matters at hand. It would never do to have Rachel Cresswell ogling a gentleman like a lovelorn schoolgirl. She did have a reputation to uphold.

Waiting until he had battled his way to her side, she offered him a smile.

"Anthony, at last," she breathed in low tones. "I feared that you must have been caught."

He shrugged, the dark gaze running an appreciative gaze over her slender form.

"We were forced into hiding on a few occasions."

"And how is she? Comfortably settled?"

"She is thoroughly delighted."

"Did you make sure that she could see well and that she could reach the platters of food that I left for her?"

"All is in order, my little g—general," he said wryly. "I would not have left her if I was not certain."

"I only wish the night to be very special for her."

"I doubt she will soon forget it. Her eyes were shining as brightly as any diamond."

"And you warned her not to lean too close to the curtains?"

He smiled deep into her wide eyes. "You know, you sound remarkably like an overbearing mother hen protecting her chick."

A sharp, unexpected pang abruptly wiped the smile from her lips.

"Nonsense."

Watching the light dim in her eyes, Anthony's brows drew together in puzzlement.

"Why should it be n—nonsense? You will someday be a wonderful mother."

"No," she said softly.

"What?"

"I will never have children."

With an impatient glance at the numerous guests that hovered near, Anthony grasped her elbow and tugged her behind a fluted column.

"Of course you shall have children," he said with more force than was necessarily warranted. Almost as if her claim annoyed him. Which was ridiculous, of course. Why should he possibly concern himself with the question of whether or not she would choose to have children? "Eventually you will put aside your absurd fears of marriage and be eager to have a family with the proper gentleman."

Rachel felt a flare of irritation at his persistence. This was not a subject she wished to dwell upon. Especially not on an evening she had worked so hard to make special.

"You do not know me as well as you think you do."

He appeared to be battling his own annoyance. "You prefer this shallow image of independence to the genuine love of a husband and children? I do not accept that, Rachel. Deep inside you wish to possess what your sisters have discovered."

Her heart clenched as his shaft slid easily home. "I am not like my sisters."

"Why?"

"They have taken after my mother," she said in pointed tones. "They are loyal and steadfast and always virtuous."

He gave a shake of his head. "What the devil are you implying?"

Rachel briefly wondered if he was being deliberately obtuse.

"I would think it was obvious that I inherited my father's unpredictable temperament."

Anthony paused as a uniformed servant halted with a tray of champagne. At his dark scowl the poor man hurriedly backed away, treading on the toe of a large matron who promptly screeched in protest.

Ignoring the chaos he had created, Anthony continued to regard Rachel with a narrowed gaze.

"You are somewhat impulsive, I will grant. But that is hardly an insurmountable fault."

"You do not understand."

"Then m—make me understand."

She heaved a sigh, silently cursing him for being so persistent. She had never discussed her inner fears with anyone. Not even Sarah or Emma.

"I love my father. And I have never doubted his love for me," she began in grudging tones.

He stepped closer to better catch her low words, his male power surrounding her.

"You are very fortunate," he murmured.

"Yes, I am, but that does not make me blind to the fact that my father's own desires and impulsive whims have ruled his life. My father will always do what is best for the Devilish Dandy. At times such behavior is very painful to those in his life."

He appeared thunderstruck at her perfectly logical explanation. Which was nonsense. Surely he had already determined himself that she was too impulsive and strong-willed to ever make a gentleman a comfortable wife?

"You are not your father," he breathed in disgruntled tones.

"But I am very much like him. I can be selfish and determined to go my own way."

His lips thinned as if annoyed by her perfectly logical explanation.

"You can also be generous, kind, and thoughtful. I know of no other maiden who would have taken such a concern in an unknown young girl."

She shrugged in a restless manner. "Anyone would feel sympathy for her plight."

"Sympathy perhaps, but few would have gone to the efforts to please her as you have."

"I have done very little," she protested.

"Good God, enough of this, Rachel," he said in stern tones, reaching out to grasp her hand in a tight grip. "I will not have you doubting your essential goodness. Whatever your father's faults, they are not yours."

A momentary doubt made Rachel hesitate. How many occasions had her sisters rued her wild nature and compared her to the Devilish Dandy? Even those in society labeled her the Devil's Daughter. She had in time accepted the comparison as undeniable. She was reckless and wild and self-indulgent. But was it possible she possessed a small measure of her mother's sweet nature as well?

"How can you be so certain?" she asked before she could halt the words.

His grip on her fingers tightened. "Because I know you. I have seen into your heart."

Just for a moment she became lost in the dark tenderness in his eyes. There was such faith in those eyes. A belief in her that she had never before experienced. Then the realization of how vulnerable her heart was becoming made her abruptly pull away from his seductive promise.

No, she told herself with a flare of fear. She was not yet prepared to ponder such dangerous thoughts.

"This is absurd."

He opened his lips to continue his argument, but

noting the wary determination of her set features he heaved a rueful sigh.

"I will convince you yet, my stubborn dove. But for now I will be content to enjoy a waltz. Shall we?"

Relieved that he was willing to drop the disturbing subject, Rachel gave a faint nod of her head.

At the moment the daring waltz seemed far safer than continuing the futile conversation.

The satin darkness settled about Rachel with a near-tangible force. Beneath the warmth of her velvet cloak she shivered, as much from unease as the brisk air.

It had been more impulse than rational thought that had led her from the comfort of her bedchamber to the dark woods that surrounded the dowager house.

She simply had to assure herself that Anthony had returned Julia to her bed without mishap, she had acknowledged. She had not fully approved of his decision to carry her back to the dowager house rather than using his carriage. Although she realized a carriage would attract undue attention, she could not help but fear that an errant guest or servant might stumble across them.

She would not possibly sleep a wink if she was forced to worry the entire night whether or not Anthony had managed to return safely.

She did not question her overriding concern for both Anthony and Julia. It was simply there and she knew she could not idly wait to find out that all was well.

Grimacing at the dampness seeping through her slippers, Rachel gathered the cloak even tighter about her, abruptly freezing at the faint rustle directly before her.

"Anthony?" she called softly. "Is that you?" A heavy silence greeted her words, then without warning a large shadow loomed before her. "Oh."

"Rachel." A familiar, highly exasperated voice sent a flare of relief through her. "What the devil are you doing out here?"

"I wanted to be certain that you returned Julia safely."

"She is being happily settled in her bed by your maid," he retorted in clipped tones.

"And she enjoyed her evening?"

"I should be very surprised if she even closes her eyes tonight for thinking of her grand adventure."

"Did you remember to tell her that she must hide her ball gown so that it will not be found by Mrs. Greene?"

"Everything is taken c—care of." He stepped close enough so that Rachel could begin to detect the tight cast of his aquiline features. "Now, my dear, we will discuss your foolishness in coming out here alone."

Unaccustomed to having her actions questioned by anyone, Rachel arched her brows.

"You are out here alone."

"It is not at all the same, as you well know."

Rachel's brows drew together at the stern warning in his voice.

"Anthony, are you attempting to lecture me?"

"I most certainly am," he retorted without the least hint of apology. "What if some man had happened by? You would have been completely at his mercy."

Rachel blithely forgot her brief moment of fear when Anthony had first appeared.

"I am quite capable of caring for myself. Indeed, I have been doing so for quite some time."

He appeared remarkably unimpressed by her prim words.

"That was because you had not yet entered my life. From now on you will take greater care of yourself. Beginning with not roaming about the countryside in the midst of night."

A fierce stab of pleasure filled her heart at his words, unnerving Rachel with its intensity.

"Sir, I believe that you overstep your bounds."

"Indeed?" Without warning he reached out to grasp her shoulders and jerked her close. Rachel opened her mouth to protest at the same moment that his head descended to capture her lips in a fierce, utterly possessive kiss. A poignant ache bloomed in the pit of her stomach. She wanted him to pull her even closer. To wrap his arms about her and kiss her until the dawn crested. But even as she instinctively swayed forward, he was lifting his head to regard her with a glittering gaze. "Now I have overstepped my bounds."

More than a little shaken by her swift, uncontrollable reaction to his unexpected kiss, Rachel pulled from his grasp.

She was not entirely certain that she cared for this power he possessed over her. Even if it did create a storm of pleasure whenever he was near.

"I believe we should return to the house."

"You are no doubt right," he agreed, circling his fingers about her elbow to steer her from the woods. For a time they walked in silence, then Anthony glanced down at her shadowed countenance. "Did you enjoy the ball?"

Rachel shrugged, recalling the evening that had been filled with a wide variety of emotions. Now that she was certain Julia was safe, she could dwell upon her earlier unease.

"I suppose it went as well as could be expected."

"Because it was a simple country ball?" he teased.

She glanced up, her expression troubled. "Because the future bride appeared grimly miserable and the future bridegroom was so puffed up with his own self-importance that he did not even notice."

"Yes," he agreed grimly, "it is a poor match."

"I am afraid for Violet," Rachel confessed, unable to banish the strange conversation she had shared with the maiden. "Her disposition is so low that I fear she might do something desperate."

"You fear she might bolt?"

Rachel hesitated, uncertain what she feared. In truth, if Violet simply decided to bolt it would be a relief, she had to acknowledge. Fleeing from an unwanted marriage might create a bit of gossip, but it would not do irrevocable harm to one's reputation.

"I do not know. She spoke to me tonight of a life of scandal. She said that she envied the freedom that scandal had brought to my life."

His grip abruptly tightened on her elbow. "Did you tell her that rather than freedom scandal has made you afraid to trust in yourself and in love?"

She stiffened at his harsh accusation. "I trust in myself."

"No, you do not. You believe because your father is fickle and undependable, you will be the same."

"It is a rather rational belief," she said tartly. "We are very much alike."

Anthony muttered a curse beneath his breath. "It is utter rubbish. Your father was free to make the choices in his life that he made, just as you are free to make your own choices. It is solely within your own power whether to be irresponsible or steady of nature."

Rachel made an impatient sound. It was very easy

for him to dismiss her fears as nonsense. He had not been raised by the Devilish Dandy. Nor lived a life of unpredictable chaos that had kept her and her sisters in constant upheaval.

"You do not believe in fate?" she demanded.

"Of course not. I believe our futures are firmly in our own hands."

"You can not be so certain."

"Yes, I can be." He brought her to a firm halt, gazing down at her with a somber expression. "Your love for your father has never wavered, despite his faults and weaknesses. And no one can doubt your attachment to your sisters."

"I love them, but that does not prevent me from doing things that they disapprove of."

He gave a short laugh. "Good gads, Rachel, d—do you not suppose that my mother disapproves of my fascination with inventions or my dislike of society?"

She wondered if he was deliberately attempting to misread her words. Surely he could not truly understand just how closely she resembled her scapegrace father.

"I have not started a school to help the poor, as Sarah has done, nor have I attempted to support myself, as Emma. I have devoted myself to frivolous concerns."

He gave a shake of his head. "I do not believe I have ever encountered a maiden more determined to give me a disgust of her."

She was taken aback by his accusation. "I am merely attempting to be truthful."

His hand gently cupped her cheek. "I know the truth, my dearest. No amount of warnings will convince me otherwise."

Her knees felt oddly weak as she gazed at the determined set of his features.

"What do you want from me?"

There was a long unnerving silence as if Anthony were uncertain himself what it was he desired. Then much to her relief he offered her a wry smile and turned to continue on their way toward Carlfield Manor.

"For tonight merely to ensure that you are safely returned to your bed. Tomorrow we will consider your most provocative question."

Twelve

The night was a long, restless one for Anthony. Over and over he had brooded about that moment he had gazed down at Rachel's moon-kissed countenance.

"What do you want from me?" she had demanded.

What, indeed.

He had been uncertain of his reason for following Rachel to Surrey. He had known he was fascinated and tantalized. He had known that he wanted to become better acquainted with her vibrant spirit. And he had known that he had to kiss those enticing lips at least once in his lifetime.

But last night he had been struck by blinding realization.

He might have followed Rachel out of some mysterious compulsion, but he had remained because he was falling in love with her.

Not surprisingly he had been stunned by the knowledge.

He had rarely given thought to acquiring a wife. As he had assured Rachel, he possessed any number of cousins who could carry on the Clarke name. And he could not conceive of a woman who would not eventually bore him to distraction. Certainly none of his mistresses had managed to produce more than a tepid interest.

But he had foolishly underestimated the potent allure of Rachel Cresswell.

Here was a woman who would never bore him.

She might drive him mad, he acknowledged wryly, but he would never be bored. And what an utterly delicious method of going batty.

A heat stirred within him even as a wry smile curved his lips.

He wanted Rachel more than he had ever wanted any woman. In truth, he burned for her with an intensity that was near painful. But his desire for her was not merely physical. He craved to see her smile, to watch her kind tenderness toward Julia, to match his wits and intelligence with her own and enjoy her ability to bewitch an entire room with one glance from those amazing hazel eyes.

Gads, he did not know how it had happened. What precise moment Rachel had tunneled her way into his heart. The only thing he was certain of was that he wanted her in his life.

Now and forever.

A wish that unfortunately was unattainable until he could convince the perverse minx that she was not doomed to make the same mistakes as her father.

Absently pacing across the library, Anthony gave a shake of his head. Somehow when dealing with Rachel things were never simple. She was a complex mystery that would take an eternity to unravel.

Reaching the window, he gazed at the brisk March rain that peppered the diamond-shaped panes. Spring had arrived in force, drenching the Surrey landscape in a flurry of brief, but violent storms.

Considering the heavy clouds with a restless frown,

Anthony was interrupted by the sound of the door to the library being pushed open.

Surprised at the interruption since most of the guests were still in their chambers dressing for dinner, Anthony turned to discover Mr. Foxworth stepping into the room. His surprise only deepened when the gentleman, elegantly attired in a cranberry coat and pink pantaloons, closed the door and deliberately turned the lock.

Turning about, the older gentleman regarded Anthony with a smooth smile.

"Good evening, Mr. Clarke."

"Mr. Foxworth."

"May I have a moment?"

Instantly intrigued, Anthony stepped from the window and gave a nod of his head.

"Certainly." He cast a deliberate glance at the closed door. "I assume this is of a private nature?"

"Yes."

Anthony smiled, regarding the lean features that were so similar to Rachel's. Over the past week he had spent more than a few moments pondering this gentleman and his obvious concern and affection for his niece.

"I do h—hope I am not to be called out. It is rumored that the Devilish Dandy is deadly on the field of honor."

A sharp silence descended before the gentleman gave a rueful grimace.

"I feared that you had learned the truth. Did Rachel tell you?"

"No. It was simply the obvious closeness between the two of you. Far closer than a mere uncle and niece. Also, she possesses many of your mannerisms."

He offered Anthony an admiring bow. "Thankfully few are as perceptive as you, Mr. Clarke."

Anthony casually leaned against the edge of the heavy walnut desk.

"Why are you in Surrey?"

The Devilish Dandy lifted his hands in a dismissive motion. "I feared my impetuous and rather headstrong daughter might manage to land herself in a bumble broth without my presence. She can be far too rash when her heart is involved."

"Do you mean her determination to have revenge on Lady Broswell?"

"Yes."

Anthony narrowed his dark eyes, hoping to discover the answer to a number of questions that had been plaguing him.

"You know, I must admit a confusion in her behavior. Rachel is n—not a petty or spiteful maiden. Why does she feel such antagonism toward Lady Broswell?"

There was a pause before the Devilish Dandy gave a small shrug.

"Because she is her aunt."

Anthony abruptly stiffened. "What?"

"My wife was sister to Lady Broswell," he retorted, the green eyes glinting at Anthony's obvious shock. "Needless to say I was not readily accepted into the family. In fact, we were forced to flee England and the family put out that Rosalind had died rather than admit she had wed so far beneath herself."

"Good God," Anthony breathed, suddenly realizing just how personal Rachel's connection to Lady Broswell truly was. It certainly explained why she had taken the woman's vindictive insults so much to heart. It also explained Lady Broswell's irrational dislike of the daughter of the Devilish Dandy. The woman would always view Rachel as a threat to her social position.

"Rachel has always resented how her mother was treated and to some measure, herself. I believe that she is determined to prove to herself that she is every bit as worthy as Lady Broswell and her daughters."

Anthony gave a slow nod of his head, his heart aching for the pain Rachel had endured at the hands of her own family. It was a pain he was intimately familiar with.

"Yes."

The Devilish Dandy watched Anthony's features tighten in anger at the thought of Rachel's family turning their back on her.

"You care for Rachel, do you not?" he asked softly.

With an effort Anthony gained command of his scattered thoughts. This gentleman was far too clever. He needed complete control of his wits to match swords with him.

The Devilish Dandy had sought him out for a purpose. And until he discovered what that purpose was he intended to be on guard.

"Are you about to demand my intentions?" he demanded.

A mocking expression descended upon the lean countenance. "I know your intentions."

"Indeed?"

"You intend to marry Rachel."

Anthony was caught off guard despite himself. Gads, he had only come to that conclusion a few hours before. How the blazes could this man have ascertained the contents of his heart?

"You sound very certain."

"If I were not so certain I would have put an end to your familiarity with Rachel days ago."

There was a dangerous edge to his voice that went a shiver down Anthony's spine. Clearly the rumors surrounding the Devilish Dandy were not exaggerated, he reluctantly acknowledged. Those green eyes held enough ruthless warning that he couldn't help but be relieved that he was not merely toying with Rachel's affections.

"Very well. I have every intention of asking Rachel to be my wife," Anthony conceded, his smile twisting as he thought of his elusive prey. "Unfortunately I am far from certain of her response."

It was the older gentleman's turn to be taken aback.

"Surely you do not doubt her love for you?"

Anthony thought briefly of Rachel's sweet response to his touch, the manner her gaze sought him out when she entered the room, and her open pleasure when in his company.

"I believe she has become attached to me," he conceded, his lips thinning with impatience when he considered her stubborn insistence never to wed. "But she has managed to convince herself she is of an unsteady temperament and incapable of being a good wife and mother."

"Unstable temperament? That is absurd," the older man scoffed.

"My thoughts precisely. Rachel, however, believes herself far too like you, sir."

Surprisingly, the Devilish Dandy flinched, as if he had been struck.

"I suppose I deserve that. I was a wretched father," he conceded in low tones. "Not only did I fail to give my daughters a proper home, but I rarely considered how my less-than-respectable behavior would reflect on them. It was only when I was obliged to spend my days staring at the nearby hangman that I truly realized just how selfish I had been. They deserved so much more than I had given them. I swore that if I was ever freed I would devote myself to ensuring they found the happiness that I did not give to them." He paused, regarding Anthony with an unwavering gaze. "I believe that you can offer Rachel that happiness."

Anthony gave a slow nod of his head. "As do I. It is just a matter of convincing Rachel."

"I do not doubt if anyone can, it is you."

Anthony took a measure of comfort from his words. Rachel could be annoyingly stubborn, but she was not stupid. Surely with a bit of encouragement she would realize her fears were groundless.

Knowing that only time would tell, he turned the conversation away from his troubles.

"Why did you seek me out?"

With an elegant motion the Devilish Dandy strolled toward the blazing fire that battled the damp chill in the air. Anthony felt his intrigue return as he detected the fine tension that stiffened the lean body.

"As I told you, I made a promise to myself when I was in Newgate that I would devote myself to my daughter's happiness," he at last murmured, slowly turning to face Anthony with a somber expression. "Rather late, I will be the first to admit, but my intentions are sincere. I have seen Sarah and Emma make suitable matches. I have only to assure myself that Rachel will be safely settled before I can live out my life in obscure retirement in a small villa I own in Italy."

Anthony raised his brows. "And so you only wished to assure yourself that I meant to propose to Rachel?"

He smiled wryly. "Not precisely."

"I thought not."

"Although my intention on coming to Surrey was merely to prevent Rachel from any outrageous antics, I have found myself extraordinarily distracted," he confessed.

It did not take a scholar to guess the identity of the older gentleman's distraction.

"Miss Carlfield?"

"Yes." He gave a humorless laugh. "For a gentleman of mature years I have become very foolish."

Anthony possessed a measure of sympathy for his companion. He was rapidly discovering that love occurred without warning and without sympathy for those it struck.

"I suppose it is my turn to inquire of your intentions toward my cousin."

"My intention was simply to offer her a means of escape from her untenable position." The Devilish Dandy left the fireplace to restlessly pace toward the towering bookcase. "I could not stand aside and watch her barter herself to a gentleman who would ruthlessly destroy her delicate spirit."

"An admirable s—sentiment," Anthony murmured, easily able to recognize the allure of a sweet, helpless maiden in dire trouble to a jaded sophisticate.

"But she refused my offers of money and even the promise to pay off her father's debts." He gave a frustrated shake of his head. "She claimed there was only one means of help that she would accept."

"And what was that?"

"Marriage."

"You intend to elope with Violet?"

"Yes." The green eyes blazed with determination. "Before you begin your protests, allow me to assure you that I have already confessed my true identity and spoken on the vast differences in our ages. I have also warned her that young maidens often imagine themselves in love with the first convenient gentle-man when they are being compelled into an unwanted marriage."

"But she refused to listen to reason?"

The Devilish Dandy grimaced. "She claims that her love is genuine and unshakable."

Although Anthony was not extraordinarily close to Violet, he did not believe she was a witless chit. She was certainly capable of knowing her own heart.

"And what are your feelings?"

"I love her," he said with a simple sincerity. "I wish to take her to Italy."

There was a determination in his voice that assured Anthony that he had made his decision and nothing would sway him from his purpose. Certainly not any protest that Anthony might raise.

"Since you are in no need of my blessing I assume there is something else you require from me?"

The lazy smile returned. "As I noted, you are very perceptive."

"What is it?"

"I intend to leave here Wednesday on the pretext of visiting nearby acquaintances. I wish for you to escort Rachel back to London on Thursday."

"It will, of course, be my pleasure to escort Rachel," Anthony agreed, his gaze narrowing. "I am curious to learn, however, how you intend to spirit Violet away from this house."

The Devilish Dandy lifted his shoulders in a non-chalant motion.

"I will return to London and arrange our travel to Italy. Next week Violet is expected to travel to stay with her cousin. Along the way she will stay at an inn. I will meet her there and we will leave during the night. By the time Mr. Carlfield realizes that she has disappeared it will be too late to halt us."

"A s—simple but no doubt effective plan," Anthony congratulated.

The older gentleman eyed Anthony squarely. "May I count on your support?"

Although Anthony was not entirely convinced that the Devilish Dandy was an appropriate husband for his young cousin, he did know that he was far preferable to Mr. Wingrove. At least she would not be browbeaten and humiliated until her soul was broken.

"I want your promise that you will treat Violet with the respect and consideration due her."

A startlingly tender expression softened the lean features. "She is more precious to me than my own life. I will do everything in my power to make her happy. And to make certain that she is not forced to remain with me out of necessity I will make provisions for a suitable allowance that will continue even if she chooses to leave Italy."

Anthony knew he could not ask for more. It was up to Violet to train this gentleman in the duties of being a proper husband. And he had an odd premonition that she was just the lady to accomplish the difficult task.

"I suppose you could be no worse than Mr. Wingrove," he conceded with a faint smile.

The Devilish Dandy offered him a sardonic bow. "Thank you."

"And I will admit to a rather reprehensible desire to know that my uncle will be forced to step from behind his daughter's skirts and accept his fate like a man."

"Yes," the Devilish Dandy agreed with a wicked smile.

"You may depend upon me," Anthony assured the older gentleman.

"Thank you." He walked to the door and turned the lock, then he glanced over his shoulder. "You will let me know when the wedding is arranged?"

Wedding.

Anthony felt his heart leap with anticipation.

"But, of course."

"Take care of Rachel. She is not nearly so invincible as she would have others believe."

"She will be cherished as the greatest treasure it has ever been my fortune to discover."

The gentleman gave a slow nod of his head, then pulling open the door, he swiftly disappeared into the hall.

Left on his own, Anthony breathed out a small sigh. Although he was not particularly dismayed at the thought of having the Devilish Dandy as a father-in-law, he was not sorry he would be soon on his way to Italy. Having one volatile, highly unpredictable Cresswell in his life was quite enough.

The thought was just passing through his mind when the sound of footsteps could be heard and Rachel herself appeared in the doorway.

As always he felt a thrill of pleasure at the mere sight of her. This evening she looked delectable in a peacock-blue satin gown, her golden curls pulled back by a matching ribbon.

He could not deny a faint hint of annoyance, however, as he noted her clear eyes and flawless skin. She obviously had not devoted her night to pacing the floor and searching her heart for the truth of her emotions as he had done. Indeed, she appeared to have slept without a care in the world.

"Good evening, Rachel."

Stepping into the room, she offered him a faint frown. "Was that my uncle who just left?"

Having determined that the Devilish Dandy did not intend to reveal his upcoming marriage to his daughter, Anthony realized he would have to guard his tongue.

"Yes."

"What were you discussing?"

Anthony shrugged in a negligent manner, hoping to ease the wariness he could sense shrouded about her.

"He has decided to leave on Wednesday to visit a few acquaintances nearby and requested that I escort you back to London on the following day."

"Acquaintances? What acquaintances?" she demanded in sharp tones.

"He did not offer any particular names and I did not feel it my place to quiz him."

"He knows no one in Surrey," she muttered. "What is he up to?"

Hoping to distract her all too quick wits, Anthony smiled in a knowing manner.

"Perhaps he is merely seeking an excuse to leave early without offending Mr. Carlfield. Your uncle is hardly the sort to enjoy rusticating in the country."

"My uncle may not enjoy rusticating in the country, but he does delight in offending others," she pointed out in dry tones. "If he wished to leave, he would make sure that Mr. Carlfield was fully aware of his reason for departing."

"Does it truly matter?"

"Yes. It is very worrisome."

He slowly strolled forward. "What is w—worrisome? The thought of having to share my carriage back to London?"

"Of course not," she denied with a hint of impatience. "I was referring to my uncle."

"He is no doubt capable of taking care of himself."

"I am not nearly so confident," she muttered, clearly disturbed at the thought of her father loosened upon the world without her restraining presence. Anthony could not entirely blame her. No doubt she worried that his rather nasty habits from the past might return and plunge him straight back to Newgate.

Barely aware of his movements, Anthony discreetly checked to make sure that he still had his valuables. Then, with an amused shake of his head at the realization that gentleman would hopefully be his father-in-law, he sought to change the subject.

"Tell me, did you visit Julia this afternoon?" he demanded.

His ploy was thankfully successful as the concern eased from her lovely face and a pleased sparkle entered the hazel eyes.

"Yes. She could speak of nothing but the ball."

"No ill effects from her late night?"

"None at all. I do believe that she has never been happier."

The vague concern that had been steadily building within Anthony brought a frown to his brow.

"A rather disturbing thought," he said softly.

Rachel blinked in surprise. "What ever do you mean?"

"In a few days we will be leaving Surrey," he pointed out with a flare of regret for the poor child. "I begin to wonder if we have done Julia a grave disservice by teaching her to expect more of her days than sitting beside the window watching others through a telescope."

A hint of uncertainty dimmed her smile as she realized the logic in his low words.

"Surely it is better to have known a few days of freedom? The memories will bring her happiness for some time."

"Or discontent as she longs for what she now knows to be out of reach. She was resigned to her life before our arrival. I wonder if we have done more harm than good."

The uncertainty deepened to dismay as Rachel considered just how bleak Julia's future would be once they were gone.

"You are right," she breathed, her eyes darkening with concern. "We must do something."

Easy enough to say, but much more difficult to accomplish, Anthony sadly acknowledged. Julia's fate belonged firmly in the hands of her family. No court would allow him to interfere, even if it did make his stomach twist to think of leaving that child in her cold, lonely house.

"What would you have us do, my dear?" he asked in sympathetic tones.

"We must confront Lady Broswell and demand that she take better care of her daughter. I now have proof that Julia does indeed belong to her."

Anthony did not question how she had gained her knowledge. He was far more concerned with keeping the fiery minx from tumbling them all into disaster.

"Rachel, such a confrontation is more likely to frighten the woman into making Julia disappear completely. At least here she is properly fed and kept safe. If she were put in an orphanage or an asylum she would be prey to every bounder that wished to abuse her."

Her hands clenched at her side as she glared into his somber countenance.

"Then what can we do?"

For once Anthony did not have a ready answer. Although he was a gentleman who easily took command of difficulties, who indeed delighted in creating the possible out of the seemingly impossible, he could think of no simple solution to the problem.

"I fear I do not know at the moment. It will take some time to consider the problem."

Her lips tightened in a dauntingly familiar manner. "I will think of something. Lady Broswell will not be allowed to make that girl suffer. She has caused enough pain for one lifetime. This time I will ensure that something is done."

Anthony heaved a sigh.

Fate no doubt found it vastly amusing that a gentleman who had always lived a calm, placid existence with few disruptions had tumbled in love with a fiery, unpredictable minx who was quite likely to drive him to Bedlam.

Thirteen

Standing in the shadows of a small alcove, Rachel carefully tracked her father's movements down the hallway and at last into the small parlor.

After two days of attempting to speak with her father in private, she had at last given up the bold approach and resorted to a more subtle method. It had taken nearly two hours of hovering in the chilled hallway, but at last her efforts had paid off.

She would have answers from her father. On this occasion he would not be allowed to slip away.

Moving across the hall, Rachel silently slipped into the room and closed the door behind her. Busy pouring himself a glass of brandy, Solomon did not realize he was no longer alone until she spoke.

"Hello, Father."

In obvious surprise he turned about to meet her narrowed gaze. It took only a heartbeat, however, for his practiced charm to return.

"Ah, good day, Rachel."

"May I have a word with you?"

"I fear I am rather occupied this afternoon."

Rachel placed her hands on her hips, not about to be dismissed after her long wait.

"You appear to be oddly occupied every afternoon," she accused.

"Yes, well, so goes the hectic life of a toasted leader of society." He gave an elegant shrug, then ran a hand down is deep-lavender coat. "Tell me, dearest, do you believe I have increased just a trifle about the waist? I accused my valet of moving the buttons, but he swears his innocence with tedious insistence. I can only suppose that he is telling the truth."

She gave a shake of her head at his deliberate attempt to distract her.

"You are precisely the same size you were yesterday, and the day before, Father. I shall not be fobbed off with your foolishness."

"Foolishness?" He sniffed in disapproval. "My dearest, I assure you that when a gentleman reaches my advanced years his waistline is of prime importance. You would not wish me waddling about like poor Prinny?"

There mere thought of her trim, always energetic father ever being as bloated as the unfortunate Prince Regent made her lips twist in reluctant amusement.

"What I wish is to discover why you are deliberately attempting to avoid me."

"Do not be a goose," he chided smoothly. "You know that I adore being with you."

"Really?" She took a deliberate step closer. "Then why are you forever disappearing the moment that I enter a room?"

"I do not disappear."

"Yes, you most certainly do."

He gave a dismissive wave of his hand. "Your imagination is running away from you. I am merely occupied with overseeing the packing of my bags and ensuring that the carriage is prepared for my departure on the morrow."

Rachel did not have to be a mind reader to realize

he was lying. Her father was a master at disappearing at a moment's notice. And his servants had been well trained to ensure that they were always prepared. In his profession his very life depended on such ability.

"Ah yes," she drawled. "You are to visit your acquaintances, are you not?"

"Yes."

"I do not believe I am familiar with these mysterious acquaintances."

A renegade flare of amusement glittered in the green eyes at her mocking tone.

"I fear there is nothing mysterious about Lord and Lady Halford. They are staid, dull, and tediously predictable country gentry. Indeed, the only thing remarkable about them is the fact that they haven't the least conversation or wit. And as for their cook"—he gave a dramatic shudder—"well, let me just say that she has yet to discover a piece of meat or fish that she can not boil to the taste of an old shoe."

Rachel did not doubt that Lord and Lady Halford were as real as Father Christmas.

"If they are so dull and their cook so unskilled, why do you wish to visit them?"

He lifted his brows as if surprised by her perfectly reasonable question.

"My dear, it would hardly be polite to be in the neighborhood and not at least pay my respects."

"Fustian. You have never concerned yourself with being polite to anyone. Indeed, you are notorious for your ill manners. Why would you care what they think of you?"

"Egads, Rachel, you begin to sound remarkably like a wretched magistrate," he complained, setting aside his untouched brandy. "Is there a particular reason for plaguing me with these endless questions?"

She met his gaze squarely. "Because I think you are lying to me."

"My dear." He pressed his hands to his heart in a gesture that was suitable for the stage. "I am wounded."

Growing increasingly annoyed with his smooth ability to feint her every thrust, Rachel tossed civility to the wind.

"Not bloody likely. What are you plotting, old man?"

The Devilish Dandy gave a sudden laugh at her peevish tone. "You know me far too well, my dear."

"Yes, I do. And I know when you are about to embark on something rash and dangerous."

He sent her a reassuring smile. "I promise that it has nothing to do with you."

She was not appeased. "Does it include Violet?"

He stilled at her abrupt question, his expression impossible to read.

"What would make you think such a thing?"

"Really, Father, it is obvious you have developed a fancy for her," Rachel retorted. "I do not believe I have ever seen you in quite such a stew over a young lady."

"I see." With exquisite care the Devilish Dandy adjusted the cuff of his coat. "Tell me, do you like Miss Carlfield?"

Rachel gave an impatient click of her tongue. "Of course I do. I have been very attached to her since her first Season in London."

"She is a remarkable young lady," he murmured.

A growing suspicion bloomed to life in Rachel's heart. Her father had always been an outrageous flirt. And while he had always been discreet she did not doubt for a moment that he was very successful in seducing any number of women. But never before had he ever spoken of one of his conquests. Certainly he had never asked her opinion. She was beginning to realize her charming, elusive father had perhaps stumbled into a situation he could not manipulate.

A rather delicious thought, she had to acknowledge with wicked humor. It would serve the devious old man right to be dancing attendance on a woman half his age.

"Far too remarkable for the likes of Mr. Wingrove," she said deliberately.

The lean features tightened with a dangerous intensity. "Yes."

"You intend to save her, do you not?"

The green eyes blazed at her soft words before his lips twisted with rueful amusement hat having been so easily baited into revealing his emotions.

"If I am able to," he confessed.

Rachel suddenly understood Violet's interest in a life of scandal. If she was correct in that assuming her father intended to spirit the young lady from beneath her father's very nose, there was no doubt that there would be a dreadful uproar. Not only would Mr. Carlfield lose his only chance to save himself from his enormous debts, but he would soon discover that his only child had irrevocably attached herself to the notorious Devilish Dandy. Not an easy blow for any gentleman to bear. He would no doubt turn his back on Violet and insist that all others do the same.

Rachel sincerely hoped that Violet considered being saved from the clutches of Mr. Wingrove worth the cost of being branded with scandal.

"What will you do?"

"I can not discuss my plans. At least not yet. Be assured that I shall let you know when all is settled."

With a faint frown Rachel moved forward to place

her hand on her father's arm. Although the Devilish Dandy always appeared invincible, she knew that he was all too human. She could not bear him taking unnecessary risks. Not when the threat of the hangman remained a distinct possibility.

"Father."

"Yes, my dear?"

"You will be careful?"

"For once I intend to take the greatest care, he assured her as he gave her hand a small squeeze. Then with a charming smile he stepped back. "Now I really must check on my valet. I can not have him shifting the buttons on any more coats."

Rachel allowed him to leave, familiar enough with his secretive nature to realize that she could not force a confession of his plans. She did, however, pause long enough to send up a silent prayer. She sensed her father would have need of every bit of his legendary skill and luck to perform his latest theft. It could not hurt to have some heavenly intervention on his side.

Rounding the corner of the house, Anthony caught sight of the familiar slender form seated on a bench in the garden. He came to a halt as he studied the delicate profile currently set into uncommonly somber lines.

For the past two days she had managed to avoid him. He realized that she had been intent on discovering her father's secret and that she had been concerned the older man might do something rash. But he also suspected that she had deliberately avoided being alone with him.

She had clearly sensed his possessive manner, he wryly acknowledged. And she was no doubt aware that he had every intention of proposing. She obviously preferred to avoid their inevitable confrontation rather than be forced to decide whether to follow her heart or to cling to her ridiculous fears.

Anthony had allowed her to elude his determined pursuit. Indeed, he understood it far too well. For years he had carried the uncertainty that his father's disappointment had lodged in his heart. It had been a long and difficult path to develop faith in himself.

Somehow he knew he would have to convince Rachel to gain her own faith.

He had waited long enough, he decided. Today Rachel would consent to be his wife or . . . well, he would toss her over his shoulder and carry her off to Scotland.

Anthony smiled ruefully at his obvious descent into madness. What sane gentleman would willingly tie himself to the daughter of the Devilish Dandy? And be determined to do so whether she wished it or not?

He gave a shrug as he moved toward Rachel. Sane or not he had made his choice. Rachel would be his.

"You are appearing rather pensive, my dear," he said softly, coming to a halt beside her.

She glanced up in surprise. "Anthony."

"Is something troubling you?"

She paused for a long moment before she heaved a heavy sigh.

"I have the oddest premonition."

"What is that?"

"That everything is about to change."

The wistful note in her voice tugged at Anthony's heart, but his determination never wavered. He could make her happy, he told himself. He would devote his entire life to that purpose.

"Is that so terrible?" he asked softly.

"I am not certain that I like the notion."

"Certainly change can be unnerving, but it can also be quite d—delightful."

"Delightful in what way?" she demanded.

"Rachel." He reached out to gently pull her to her feet. For a moment he debated whether to propose first and kiss her after her agreement, or go straight for the kiss. Then the sound of approaching footsteps intruded into the peace of the garden. "Damn. I wish to speak with you. Will you take a stroll with me?"

She hesitated a long moment, then clearly sensing his unyielding determination, she gave a slow nod of her head.

"If you wish." She allowed him to take her arm and lead her from the garden. In silence they crossed the parkland, then as they entered the fringe of trees she glanced to his set countenance. "Are we going to visit Julia?"

"No, not today, I think," he murmured, steering her deeper into the dappled shadows.

"You are very quiet. Is something the matter?"

Coming to a halt, he firmly turned her to face him. Absurdly he felt a faint flutter of nerves deep in his stomach. He had never proposed before. He sincerely hoped he did not make a hash of it.

"You could say that, I suppose."

"What is it?"

"Actually it is you."

The haze eyes widened at his blunt retort. "Me?"

"Do not look so surprised, my dove." His hands absently stroked the line of her shoulders. "You are well aware that you have been leading me a merry chase. It was only a matter of time before I was firmly captured."

She stiffened with a wary unease, her tongue peeking out to wet her dry lips. "I suppose you are teasing me?"

"N—no. I have never been so serious in my entire life."

He heard her breath catch at his low words.

"I think perhaps we should return to the house."

His hand tightened on her shoulders. "I have never know you to be a coward before, Rachel."

As expected, his insult scraped at her staunch pride. "I am not a coward. I merely wish to return to the house."

"No, you wish to avoid discussing our future," he retorted in stern tones. "You do not want to admit that something magical is happening between us."

He felt her shiver even as she jutted out her chin in a stubborn motion.

"Magical? Is that your way of implying you desire to lure me into an affair?"

He resisted the urge to shake a bit of sense into her. Blast, but she could be difficult when she wished to be.

"If I wished an affair you would even now be my mistress and I would not be spending every deuced night pacing the floor."

His bold claim made her lips part in shock. "You are very confident in your skills, sir."

"Can you deny that had I been bent upon seduction I would most certainly be your lover by now?"

A surprising hint of color stained her cheeks as she struggled to evade the truth.

"Many gentlemen have attempted to seduce me."

"But has one ever stirred your passions?" he relentlessly demanded. "I have only to touch you to feel you shiver in response. Has any other gentleman ever made you feel in this manner?"

His hands shifted, trailing up the curve of her neck and lightly along the line of her jaw.

"Please," she said softly. "I can not think when you do that."

Anthony's entire body tingled with the sharp-edged pleasure he always felt when he touched this woman.

"Admit the truth, Rachel. You desire me."

For a moment Anthony feared that she might refuse to acknowledge the searing heat that simmered between them. Then the heavy lashes fluttered downward.

"Very well," she grudgingly whispered. "I will admit that I have never before felt as I do when you kiss me."

"And if I wanted to seduce you I could have," he persisted.

"Perhaps."

His fingers moved of their own will to race the softness of her lips.

"But I do not desire an affair, Rachel. I have known from the beginning that this was no passing fancy. This is no flare of lust that will swiftly die."

In a sudden panic her gaze flew upward. "You do not know what you are saying. Of course it will die."

"I am not a callow schoolboy that allows his p— passions to rule his heart," he retorted with rising impatience. "Certainly I want you in my bed, but I also want you seated across from me while I eat my breakfast and close beside me when I ride in my carriage and growing heavy with my child."

She abruptly slipped from his grasp, her hand pressed to her heart.

"You must stop this."

He relentlessly followed her retreat. "Why?"

"I have told you that I shall never wed."

"You must realize that you are being nonsensical."

"It is not nonsensical."

"Yes, it is." His gaze bore deep into her wide eyes,

willing her to realize he was not to be turned aside by her absurd notions. "You are far too intelligent to allow insubstantial fears of what you may or may not do in the future to ruin your life." He abruptly reached out to grasp her hand and pressed it to the erratic beat of his heart. "Tell me what you fear, Rachel. Is it me?"

She appeared genuinely startled by his question. "Of course not."

"Then what is it?"

Her fingers splayed against the thin lawn shirt, testing the heat of his chest. Anthony shuddered in response.

"I am afraid of hurting you."

Anthony briefly closed his eyes as he regained command of his renegade body. He would not seduce Rachel into marriage. She would agree to his proposal of her own free will.

"There will no doubt be occurrences when you do hurt me," he said in gentle tones. "Just as there will b—be occasions when I unwittingly hurt you. I do, after all, have an annoying habit of disappearing to my workroom and I am not as romantically inclined as some maidens might desire."

A small but genuine smile tugged at her lips. "Yes, there is that."

His heart leaped beneath her hand as he sensed her initial panic beginning to subside.

"I am also faithful and extraordinarily loyal to those I love. You will never want for anything as my wife."

"Wife." She tasted the word slowly, almost as if she were trying it on for size.

"It does have an appealing ring to it, does it not?" he questioned in husky tones.

"Anthony."

Her hand raised from his heart to tentatively touch his cheek. A warm tide of relief surged through Anthony at the revealing motion. It was the sign of surrender he had been waiting for.

A low groan rumbled in his throat and his arms reached out to wrap about her so he could at last claim the kiss he had longed to savor, but before he could lower his head a shrill giggle tore through the silence and Rachel was abruptly spinning away.

"What was that?"

Anthony heaved a frustrated sigh. Gads, would he ever get his kiss?

"I believe our mysterious ghosts have returned," he muttered, wishing them in Jericho.

He was on the point of suggesting they return to the house when he realized that Rachel was paying him no heed. With undisguised curiosity she impulsively plunged through the underbrush in the obvious intention of discovering the owner of the ill-timed giggle. Anthony swallowed a curse, already suspecting precisely what Rachel was about to discover.

"Rachel, no."

"I wish to discover who it is," she called softly, darting between the thick trees.

"Wait," he commanded, already in swift pursuit.

He was not swift enough, however, and as he rounded a large bush he discovered Rachel standing in frozen shock.

"Bloody hell," he muttered, giving only a brief glance to the couple locked in a passionate embrace upon a blanket before dragging Rachel away. She stumbled in silence beside him until he at last forced her to sit upon a fallen tree at the edge of the woods.

"Rachel, look at me."

She slowly lifted her darkened gaze to his pale countenance.

"That man. He was a servant?"

"Yes," he admitted in tight tones, recalling the livery coat that had been tossed on the ground.

"Do you know, I had begun to feel a measure of sympathy for Mary," she said in soft tones, destroying Anthony's vague hope that she had not had the opportunity to recognize the young woman who had been with the servant. "Lord Newell is a weak, selfish gentleman with no love for her."

"Rachel, this is none of our concern," he said firmly, cursing the ill fate that had brought the indiscreet lovers to the woods on this afternoon.

"Of course it is." She lifted her head, a bit of color returning to her pale cheeks. "Lord Newell believes Mary to be a virtuous maid. For all we know she might already be carrying the child of that man."

"It is between Lord Newell and Miss Hamlin," he said, his brows lowering as she absently nibbled on her full bottom lip. "Did you hear me, Rachel? This matter is a private affair."

Without warning she abruptly rose to her feet, a distinct glow of battle in her hazel eyes.

"Not any longer."

Anthony's heart sunk at the crisp determination in her voice.

"Rachel, what are you plotting?"

She smiled with a sweet innocence that sent a cold chill down his spine.

"I have just been struck with the most amazing notion. It will solve everything."

Anthony stepped back, throwing his hands up in the air.

"Dear God, save me from the plots of Cresswells."

Fourteen

Rachel dressed carefully the next morning, girding herself for battle with great attention to detail. For once she ignored the brilliant gowns that shimmered in the morning sunlight, choosing instead a muted rose gown with a black spencer trimmed with rose velvet ribbons. Tying a rose bonnet on her curls, she retrieved the brooch she had discovered in the woods and dropped it into her reticule. Once assured she looked the role of a determined lady of business, she slipped from the quiet house and made her way through the garden.

She sucked in a deep breath of the spring-scented air as she headed directly for the parkland. Although she was confident in her scheme, she knew that it would take every bit of her courage and skill to succeed. She had, in fact, devoted the entire night to rehearsing precisely what she would say when she reached Broswell Park.

Well, perhaps not the entire night, she conceded with a tingle of excitement. At least a part of the long night had been spent recalling Anthony's lovely proposal.

Who would have thought such an intelligent, charming, utterly delectable gentleman would ever fall in love with her? Or that he would be so determined to make her his wife?

For so long she had lived for the moment, unwilling to consider the future out of fear that she would see the stark loneliness that awaited her. But Anthony had changed all that. He had forced her to consider a future with him. A future that included a husband and children. A future filled with love.

He believed in her, she had slowly acknowledged with a thrill of warmth. He believed that she was not doomed to follow in the footsteps of her father. That she could become as steadfast and loyal as her mother. And it was that faith that had slowly stirred a belief in herself.

It was true that she possessed her father's reckless spirit, but she also possessed an unwavering love to those she held dear.

And she did love Anthony Clarke.

Her steps felt lighter as she crossed the parkland, just thinking of the man who had so disrupted her life.

He was simply everything a woman could possibly desire in a gentleman, she acknowledged. He was kind, he possessed a clever wit, and he made her feel the most wicked sensations when he was near. He had also revealed his extraordinary patience when he had been with Julia. He would make a wonderful husband and father.

The thought of Julia abruptly brought her back to her senses.

She would have ample opportunity to moon over the pleasure of possessing Anthony as a husband, she sternly lectured herself. This morning she needed to concentrate on her upcoming confrontation with Lady Broswell. She was not foolish enough to underestimate the wily old woman. It would not be a simple matter to outwit her.

Stepping into the fringe of the woods, Rachel absently opened her reticule to ensure she had the brooch with her. She knew that having such tangible proof of Mary's infidelity would be vital.

It was the rustle of leaves beside her that abruptly brought her head up. Her heart skipped a beat as a shadow fell across the path, then a large form emerged from behind a tree.

She stepped back, but as her gaze caught sight of a familiar black coat and perfect shoulders her fear melted to a fond exasperation.

"Anthony, you nearly scared me witless."

There was no apology on his handsome countenance as he regarded her in a stern manner.

"I thought you might be passing by here this morning."

She heaved an inward sigh. She had managed to avoid his attempts to coerce her into confessing her plans last evening by the simple means of retiring to her chambers. She should have realized that he would not give up his pursuit so easily.

She smiled as she realized that she would have to recall this unfortunately tenacious tendency of his in the future. He would not be an easy husband to fool.

"Why are you skulking in these woods?"

His arms crossed his chest in an ominous manner. "I wished to speak with you."

Rachel ignored the hint of warning in his voice. She was not about to discuss her plans with Anthony. At least not until she was certain she had succeeded. This was the last thing she intended to do completely on her own. She owed it to her mother. For her memory Rachel would make sure that another poor girl did not suffer her fate.

"I fear it will have to wait," she said in brisk tones. "I have an appointment this morning."

The dark eyes narrowed. "No, it can not wait."

She gave an impatient click of her tongue. "Really, Anthony, I will be less than an hour. Whatever you have to say can surely wait."

"No."

There was no mistaking his tone of voice and Rachel resigned herself to the notion she would have to hear him out.

Not that she minded spending time with her beloved, she silently acknowledged. The mere sight of him was enough to make her stomach quiver in the most fascinating fashion. But she preferred to have her business over and done with so that she could concentrate on this gentleman with no further distractions.

"Very well," she conceded. "What is it?"

"I think you should know that I have spoken with your father."

It was not at all what she had been expecting and she instinctively stiffened in alarm.

"My father?"

"Yes. I know that your uncle Foxworth is in truth the Devilish Dandy."

"I see."

As always he easily read the wariness in her eyes. He offered her a reassuring smile.

"Do not worry. I have no intention of revealing his identity. After all, I have no desire to have my father-in-law lodged in Newgate."

In truth Rachel had not for a moment feared Anthony would reveal her father. She was far more concerned that he would be angered by their charade.

"What did you discuss?"

"Your strange obsession to have revenge on Lady Broswell."

"I have already explained my reasons."

He stepped closer, his all too knowing eyes searching her guarded expression.

"You failed to mention that Lady Broswell is your aunt."

Rachel could not disguise her shock. "My father told you that?"

"I believe he wished me to understand your anger." His expression abruptly softened. "And I do understand, Rachel. It is not p—pleasant to be considered an embarrassment to your own family."

"No, it is not," she agreed, although she was surprised to discover she felt none of the pain she normally experienced when she thought of her aunt and her cold dismissal of her own sister's family.

"I also understand the desire to strike back at those who have treated you with less respect than you deserve. But I assure you, my dear, that revenge is a hollow victory."

"This is not revenge," she denied. "This is justice."

His lips thinned. "Do you intend to reveal Mary's indiscretion to her mother?"

"Yes," Rachel admitted, refusing to lie.

"And you claim that it is justice?"

"It will be."

"No, it will not. Justice is righting a wrong, not striking out to wound another because they have wounded you."

She met his gaze steadily. "I intend to right a wrong."

"Rachel," he muttered in impatience, reaching out to grasp her upper arms.

Leaning forward, Rachel placed her hands upon the

solid strength of his chest, breathing deeply of his warm scent.

"Tell me, Anthony, did you mean what you said yesterday?"

The dark eyes abruptly smoldered with a satisfying desire.

"When I said that I wanted you to be my wife?"

"Yes."

"Of course I m—meant it," he growled. "I want you to be in my life for an eternity."

Rachel smiled. An eternity. At the moment it did not seem nearly long enough.

"That is what I want as well."

He groaned deep in his throat as his arms wrapped about her and squeezed her tight enough to make her fear for her ribs.

"Good God, you do not have any notion of how happy you have made me."

"No happier than myself," she confessed, laying her head against his chest so she could hear the thunderous beat of his heart. "For so long I have believed I would always be alone. Now I can not conceive of a future without you."

He slowly pulled back so he could view her delicately flushed features.

"That was never to be. From the moment I saw you in the opera house you have belonged to me."

"I will no doubt drive you mad upon occasion," she could not resist warning him.

His lips twitched. "No doubt."

"And you will not be allowed to disappear into your workroom without me."

"I would not countenance it." His hand moved tantalizingly down to her lower back. "There is a very comfortable sofa in there that I believe will be perfect for the project I intend to devote my attention to for the next several years."

She shivered. "Anthony."

"Do I shock you?"

"Nothing shocks the daughter of the Devilish Dandy," she assured him, her smile filled with promise.

A sudden heat flared along the lines of his cheekbones. "Gads, I do not think I can bear to wait for the banns to be read. Still, I suppose you will desire a proper wedding?"

"Proper?" She wrinkled her nose in distaste. "Good heavens, no. I do have a reputation to uphold. I would far prefer to elope."

He gave a pleased chuckle. "I believe a special license is as daring as I wish to be."

Rachel heaved a teasing sigh. "I knew that you would be wretchedly respectable."

"Does that disappoint you?"

She gazed deep into his dark eyes. "Not as long as you love me."

"Forever." He loosened his grip so he could lift a hand and gently cup her cheek. "Shall we return to the house? I have a great deal to accomplish if we are soon to be wed."

Rachel smiled wryly as she stepped backward. She did not wish to battle with her brand new fiancé, but she was determined to finish her business with Lady Broswell.

"I must visit Broswell Park first. There is something I must do."

"Dash it all, Rachel," he growled. "I thought you had given up this ludicrous notion."

"Anthony, you said that you loved me. Do you trust me?" she demanded with soft insistence.

Caught in a web of his own making, he offered her a rueful smile.

"Of course I do."

"Then wait for me here. I will soon return."

"Wait." He held up a slender hand. "If you are determined to go through with this then I will come with you."

"No. I must do this on my own."

"Rachel."

"Trust me."

He briefly closed his eyes as he gave a shake of his head. "Gads, I will no doubt regret this. You are a very bad influence on me."

"I do try."

With a teasing glance she moved to brush her lips over his own before spinning away and heading up the path.

Feeling very much like one of the caged lions he had once witnessed in the Tower of London, Anthony paced through the small opening with increasing impatience.

Damn. He should never have allowed Rachel to go without him.

It was not that he feared for her safety. Lady Broswell might be a heartless, shallow witch, but she was not violent. And he certainly had no concern for the shock and embarrassment the Broswell family was about to receive. They more than deserved whatever revenge Rachel might choose to dish out.

What bothered him was the fear that Rachel would soon deeply regret striking out in anger. He knew better than anyone that in time her tender heart would be struck with remorse. He feared that she did not realize the high cost of revenge.

On the point of giving in to his impulse to leave the woods and physically remove her from Broswell Park, Anthony breathed a sigh of relief as he heard the rustle of approaching footsteps. With jerky movements he moved up the path, grasping his headstrong fiancée's arms the moment she came into view.

"Rachel, what the devil took you so long?"

Appearing far more pleased than he had expected, she smiled into his anxious eyes.

"Forgive me, but there were a few delicate negotiations that had to be taken care of."

He searched her beautiful countenance in confusion. "Negotiations?"

"Yes."

She held up a folded sheet of paper. Stepping back, Anthony took the paper from her, opening it to reveal a hastily scribbled note signed at the bottom by Lady Broswell.

"What is this?"

"It is Lady Broswell's written permission to give me custody of Julia."

A sharp stab of shock flared through him. "What?"

"I told you that I was going to Broswell Park for justice," she said, her tone triumphant. "I used my knowledge of Mary's relationship with the servant to force my aunt to give me custody of Julia."

"Good God," he breathed.

Rachel's smile faded as her eyes darkened with sudden concern. "Are you angry? I know I said nothing of my plans when you asked me to marry you. It will not be easy to interrupt your life with both a wife and a young girl."

"I would be very happy to have Julia with us,"

he eased her fears, quite prepared to bring the girl into his home. Indeed, he had been considering his own means of removing Julia from Lady Broswell's callous care. "But, my dear, this is not a legal document."

Her smile readily returned. "I shall have it made legal as soon as I return to London."

"Lady Broswell could easily change her mind," he warned.

"Not as long as she wishes Mary's indiscretion to remain a secret from Lord Newell."

He arched his brows. "That, my dear, is blackmail."

She wrinkled her nose. "Reprehensible, I know. But I could not leave here knowing Julia was trapped in that horrid place. She is my cousin, Anthony. She deserves better."

Anthony felt a surge of pride rush through him. She had promised him that she wanted justice, not revenge. And that was precisely what she had achieved. She had rescued Julia from Lady Broswell's cold control and ensured that she would be given the care she ought to have.

"How did Lady Broswell react to your demands?"

A revealing shudder shook her body as she recalled the no-doubt fiery confrontation.

"She was furious that I had learned the truth about Julia, of course. Clearly she assumed no one would ever discover that she had hidden her own daughter in the dowager house. Surprisingly, however, she was much less shocked when I revealed Mary's affair. I believe she must have suspected the truth."

Anthony gave a slow nod of his head. "Which is no doubt the reason why she is so eager for the wedding to take place between her daughter and Lord Newell."

"Yes. It took little effort after my revelation to convince her that Julia would be better in our care."

Anthony's heart leaped. "Our care." Simple words, and yet they captured the very essence of his deep happiness. He would not longer be alone. From today onward his life and heart would be entwined with this beautiful, passionate, maddening woman.

"You were right," he said, moving forward to gently wrap her in his arms. "You do have a great deal of the Devilish Dandy in you."

"Are you very angry with me?" she asked softly.

"No." He smiled as her body fitted perfectly against his own. Surrounded by the peace of the woods, with the scent of sweet roses and spring sunlight peaking through the trees, he was certain he could stay in this precise spot forever. "Although I intended a less spectacular means of rescuing Julia, you appear to have settled matters quite handily."

"It did seem the perfect solution."

"And your honor is satisfied?" he demanded. "No more plots for revenge?"

"Actually, I forgot my plot for revenge sometime ago."

"Indeed?"

The hazel eyes sparkled in an enticing manner. "Yes, I kept being interrupted by a tall, handsome gentleman who kisses me in the most amazing fashion."

Anthony sucked in a sharp breath, discovering his ability to concentrate was directly connected to her tiny wiggles to press even closer. With each wiggle his thoughts became more difficult to maintain. He would have to make sure that the minx did not use such tactics to always have her way with him. He could not be forever under her delicate heel.

She gave another wiggle and all fear of being properly henpecked disappeared.

For the moment he was quite content to be deliciously distracted.

"He sounds fascinating," he murmured.

She coyly batted her long lashes. "Utterly fascinating."

"Precisely the sort of gentleman you should marry with all possible h—haste."

"Oh, I intend to."

He gave a low chuckle, forcing himself to drop his arms and take a step backward. Although he had always been a gentleman of cool control and meticulous reason, he did not trust himself to remain alone with Rachel. He intended their wedding to be perfect, even if it was by special license. And that included their wedding night.

"Come, my minx. Let us go collect Julia before I forget we are not yet wed."

She wrapped her arm through his, leaning her head upon his shoulder as he steered them toward the dowager house. They walked in peaceful silence for some time, then without warning Rachel heaved a small sigh.

"What is it, my dear?" he asked with a faint frown.

"I wish my father was still here."

"Why?"

"I should wish him to know that we are to be wed."

Anthony's frown cleared as he smiled into her darkened eyes. "I would wager that he suspected our marriage long before we did. He is a very perceptive gentleman."

She considered his words for a long moment then gave a delighted laugh.

"Perceptive and far too sly for his own good. I

am glad he is about to endure a bit of his own medi-
cine."

"What?"

"Never mind." Her head returned to his shoulder.
"We have our own family to think of now."

Fifteen

The large town house set in an elegant square was renowned as much for its amusing peculiarities as for its notable view of the park. One could never be certain what sort of invention would be displayed in the library or even blocking the front hall. There were coatracks carved in the shape of a butler, a mirror framed by candles that was blindingly bright, and a mechanical bird that perched on the mantel and sang Rachel's favorite tune.

And of course there were the delicious rumors that the pretty Julia was a by-blow of the Devilish Dandy and that he could routinely be seen slipping through the neighborhood in the dead of night to visit his daughters.

After a year of the gossip and speculation, Rachel paid little heed to the absurd stories. Certainly they had not harmed either her or Anthony's standing in society. Indeed, it was considered a triumph of the highest order to receive a rare invitation to the Clarke town house. But more importantly, she discovered herself deliciously, wickedly, irrevocably happy.

Even standing at the bay window searching for signs of Julia's return she felt an acute flare of pleasure race through her.

Anthony had proved to be all she could ever have

hoped for in a husband. He was considerate, humorous, and a tender lover. And while their occasional battles were spectacular to behold, like two fencer's swords meeting in a shower of sparks, their inevitable reconciliation was equally spectacular. And just as importantly he had proved to be a wonderful father to Julia.

Away from the grim Mrs. Greene and encouraged to discover all the delights of London, she had blossomed into a beautiful and utterly charming young lady. Not even the disappointment at discovering that the London doctors could do nothing to help her walk had dimmed her enthusiasm to experience all that life had to offer.

An enthusiasm that had occasionally tested Rachel's nerves to the very limit.

The thought of Julia brought Rachel's wandering mind back to the matters at hand and she gazed down the busy street for the hundredth time. She had known from the beginning it was a poor notion to allow Julia out of the house without her. Anything might have happened. Who would take care of the poor girl if she were not near?

Pressing her nose to the pane, Rachel was so intent on her anxious survey that she failed to hear the door of the drawing room open and softly close. It was not until warm, wonderfully familiar arms circled her waist that she realized she was no longer alone.

"Good Lord, Rachel, you have been standing at this window for the better part of an hour."

She instinctively leaned back against the strength of her husband's broad chest.

"And I will continue to remain here until Julia returns."

He gave a low chuckle as he dropped a kiss on her golden curls.

"She is perfectly safe in the hands of Mr. Eastgate. What could possibly happen in the middle of Hyde Park?"

Rachel brooded darkly on the young gentleman who had arrived at her doorstep earlier in the day. Granted, he had appeared suitable enough. His attire had been well cut without the foolishness of a dandy and his manner of concern for Julia had seemed sincere. But Rachel was far from convinced that he was a proper companion for her young cousin.

There had been something just a trifle shifty in his narrow eyes and a weakness to his chin that she could not wholly admire.

"We know very little of this Mr. Eastgate," she pointed out in tight tones. "What if he decides to prove his skill with the ribbons and overturns them?"

Anthony's arms tightened about her. "I spoke quite sternly to the young gentleman before they left. I assure you that he was properly terrified."

"I trust you also warned him that Julia is a proper lady?"

"Of course, my dearest. Just as you commanded."

There was no mistaking the amusement laced through his obedient words. With a frown Rachel turned in his arms to regard him in a dangerous manner.

"May I ask what is so amusing?"

His lips twitched as he studied her darkened eyes. "For a woman who feared that she was too unpredictable to be a good wife and mother you have proven to be remarkably predictable in your concern for Julia."

She grimaced in a rueful manner. It was true that she had become deeply protective of Julia. She simply could not bear to think of the girl being hurt, or even disappointed.

"She is very young," she murmured.

"She is old enough to enjoy a few light flirtations. I will see that it goes no further. At least not until she has tumbled madly in love with the proper gentleman."

Knowing that he was once again right and that she was overreacting to a simple ride in the park, Rachel flashed him a provocative smile.

"By then we shall no doubt have another child to fret over."

The dark eyes flared with a smoldering passion that had not dissipated over the past year.

"I certainly intend to give my full attention to making such an event a reality."

His hands cupped her hips to pull her close and she gave a breathy laugh.

"Mr. Clarke, you are shameless."

"Only with my beautiful wife."

Rachel shivered in anticipation. "I suppose you wish to convince me that you have some project that desperately needs our attention in the workroom?"

Over the past year the small workroom had become their sanctuary. It was an unspoken rule that whenever Mr. and Mrs. Clarke disappeared to work on a project that they were not to be disturbed for any reason. Not even a raging fire or the arrival of Napoleon on their doorstep would induce the servants to consider tapping on the door.

"Well, the thought did cross my mind," he breathed, his head lowering to brush his lips over hers in a tantalizing promise.

Rachel's arms lifted to encircle his neck, but even as his lips stroked the line of her jaw there was the distant sound of the front-door knocker echoing through the house. Rachel pulled back with an expression of surprise.

"Who ever could that be?"

Anthony grimaced as he reluctantly straightened his cravat. "Someone with a most extraordinaryly poor sense of timing."

Within moments a sour-faced butler stepped into the room, his stiff formality in direct contrast to the eccentric household.

"Lady Chance and Lady Hartshore to see Mrs. Clarke."

A flare of pleasure shot through Rachel. She knew both her sisters would soon be traveling to their country seats so they could await the arrival of their babies. She cherished every opportunity to be with them while they remained in London.

"Show them in, Fisher."

"At once."

"And ask Mrs. Center to prepare tea."

"Very good."

With stiff movements the butler backed from the room.

Anthony heaved a rueful sigh. "I see I shall have to visit the workroom on my own."

Rachel sent him a teasing smile. "You could stay for tea."

"As much as I adore your sisters, three Cresswells at one time is a bit much for even my steady nerves."

"Coward."

"Sensible," he argued, dropping a light kiss on her nose. "I shall no doubt be closeted away for the remainder of the afternoon. You are welcome to join me when your guests have taken their leave."

She tilted her head to one side, as if pondering his offer. "I shall consider it. I am quite busy, of course. There was a particular bonnet I wished to purchase today, and I have yet to discuss the menu for our soirée with Cook."

"Indeed." He lowered his head to give her a brief, searing kiss. "Just something to help in your considerations."

With a glance that promised all sorts of wicked delights, Anthony turned to stroll through a narrow door at the far end of the room, disappearing into the workroom that Rachel shared on a regular basis.

She smiled at the knowledge that he would be patiently awaiting her. It was a knowledge she carried deep in her heart at all times.

The sound of approaching footsteps had her turning back to the main doorway and she watched in pleasure as her sisters swept into the room.

Much had changed in the past year. Both women were already showing the fact that they would soon present their ecstatic husbands with heirs, but the change went deeper than that.

Sarah had softened and mellowed under the influence of Lord Chance, while Emma sparkled with an unmistaken happiness that could be directly attributed to Lord Hartshore.

"Sarah. Emma." Rachel moved to give each a swift hug. "How wonderful to see you."

"Rachel, you look as beautiful as ever," Emma said, glancing about the empty room. "Where is Julia?"

Not surprisingly, both Sarah and Emma had become as fiercely attached to Julia as Rachel.

"Anthony allowed her to go for a drive with Mr. Eastgate," Rachel admitted in disapproving tones. "I am not at all convinced that he did not make a grievous error in judgment."

Sarah reached out to pat her hand, as always utterly sensible.

"I am certain she will be well. From all accounts

Mr. Eastgate is a somber, wholly sensible young gentleman."

"He had best be," Rachel muttered.

"I do wish you would allow her to come and stay with me," Emma said, attempting to distract her from her obvious concern. "She would no doubt enjoy Hartshore Park. And certainly she would be given a bit more freedom to enjoy herself there."

Rachel planted her hands on her hips as she met her sister's teasing gaze.

"You may tell me how to be a mother once your child is born."

Emma held up a hand as she smiled gently at her fiery sibling.

"Actually I was thinking of you, Rachel. You have yet to have any time alone with your husband."

Rachel's expression immediately softened at the mention of Anthony. It was always the same. Just the thought of him filled her with joy.

"Anthony makes sure that we have ample opportunity to be alone."

Sarah regarded her faint hint of color with indulgent satisfaction.

"I must say that marriage agrees with you, Rachel. I have never seen you look more content."

"I have never been happier. Anthony is quite remarkable."

"I believe that we have all been quite fortunate in our choices," Emma agreed.

Rachel gave a sudden laugh, remembering back to the years they had traveled from hotel to hotel, always in fear of being captured and never quite feeling as if they belonged anywhere.

They had come a considerable distance from their Gypsy ways.

"Who would have thought the daughters of the

Devilish Dandy would capture the most eligible bachelors in all of England?"

"Certainly not I," Emma admitted with a charming grimace. "I was quite content to live out my life as a paid companion. It was only Lord Hartshore's persistence that forced me to alter my opinion."

"Ah yes," Sarah said in dry tones. "I do believe we can safely say that all three gentlemen are remarkably persistent."

"You mean obnoxiously stubborn," Rachel corrected.

"In the most charming fashion," Emma chimed in.

The three burst into laughter as the door was pushed open and the housekeeper bustled in with a large silver tray.

"Tea, Mrs. Clarke."

"Thank you."

Moving to where the servant set the tray on a sofa table, Rachel settled her sisters on comfortable chairs before busying herself with filling them both with generous servings of delicate sandwiches and apple tarts. Once assured they were well fed and adequately revived with the strong China tea, Rachel sat back and regarded them with a hint of curiosity.

"Now, tell me what brings you here today."

"Actually, I haven't the faintest notion," Emma retorted, her own gaze shifting toward her older sister. "Sarah arrived at my doorstep insisting we must visit you this afternoon."

Rachel's curiosity deepened. "Well, Sarah?"

Sarah offered them a dimpled smile as she calmly sipped her tea.

"I wished to have us together today because I received a letter from Father this morning."

"Good heavens, where is he?" Rachel demanded, more than a little peeved he had not once visited her in the past year. Although he was always erratic and prone to coming and going without warning, he had never been gone for such a length of time.

"Italy," Sarah retorted.

Emma gave a loud choke of surprise. "Whatever is he doing there?"

"It appears that he purchased a villa near Florence some years ago. He is now living there with his new wife."

Emma dropped her cup onto the low table with a loud clatter. "Wife?"

Rachel, however, was far less surprised than her sister. She had suspected long ago that Violet would never run off with her father without being properly wed. And, of course, despite his scandalous habits, the Devilish Dandy would never compromise a young maiden of good breeding.

"Violet Carlfield," she murmured with a knowing smile.

Sarah gave a slow nod of her head. "Yes."

"Who the devil is Violet Carlfield?" Emma demanded in confusion.

"Actually, she is a friend of mine," Rachel admitted.

Emma's astonished emerald eyes widened in shock. "He wed a woman young enough to be his daughter?"

Rachel briefly recalled her father's expression as he spoke of Violet. She did not doubt for a moment that he was sincerely devoted to the sweet-tempered maiden.

"Violet is young, but I believe she is well suited to make Father a good wife," she said.

"As do I," Sarah agreed with a distinct twinkle in her eyes. "He writes that he will be a new father by the end of August."

There was a stunned silence at the unexpected announcement, then Emma sank back in her chair.

"Oh my."

Rachel gave a shake of her head, then suddenly laughed in delight.

"Good heavens, I hope it is a girl. Can you imagine unloosening another Devilish Dandy upon the world?"

Sarah joined in her laughter. "Heaven forbid."

Emma gave a disbelieving shake of her head. "I do not believe there will ever be another Devilish Dandy. He is one of a kind."

The three sisters nodded their heads in silent agreement. Solomon Cresswell was indeed an original. The world would never see his like again.

"At least he is not alone," Sarah said in practical tones. "With the three of us wed, he would have no doubt have been at loose odds without his role of matchmaker."

"And we all know the dangers of having Father at loose ends," Rachel pointed out.

"It has been quite a year," Emma said in soft tones.

"A wonderful year," Sarah concurred.

With a satisfied motion Emma touched the growing curve of her stomach.

"And it is bound to become even more wonderful."

Rachel surged to her feet, feeling as if a celebration was deserved for their boundless good fortune.

"Although it is only tea, I propose a toast to the daughters of the Devilish Dandy."

Her sisters readily rose to their feet and held out their cups so that they could tap them together.

"Here, here," Emma echoed.

"And to the future little Cresswell in Italy," Rachel

added with a smile at the thought of her father's, no doubt, amazement.

Taking a sip of her tea, Emma set aside her cup and wrinkled her nose in a rueful manner.

"I do hate to bring an end to our afternoon, but I promised Lord Hartshore that I would return home in ample time to rest before dinner. He has become quite overbearing when it comes to my health."

Sarah heaved a sympathetic smile. "Yes, gentlemen seem to lose what few wits they possess when a woman is carrying their potential heir."

Rachel briefly allowed herself to ponder her own growing suspicion she was in the same family way as her sisters. She had said nothing, not wishing to raise Anthony or Julia's hopes. And of course she knew that Anthony would be utterly irrational once he discovered her delicate condition. He would no doubt worry himself into a nervous wreck, refusing to allow her to do anything more than sit in her bed. For the time being she intended to hug her secret to herself.

Moving forward, Rachel gave Sarah a hug. "When you write to Father you will send my love?"

"Of course," she agreed, squeezing Rachel tightly before stepping back.

Rachel turned to give Emma a hug as well. "Take care, my dear."

"You will remember to give some thought to Julia coming with me to Hartshore Park?" Emma demanded. "Lady Hartshore would be delighted to have a young person about, and of course she would keep me company when Lord Hartshore is seeing to the estate. I do promise to take the best of care of her."

"I will think upon it," Rachel replied in evasive tones, unable to contemplate her home without Julia's bright presence.

With a minimum of fuss the two women swept from the room. At the same moment Rachel heard the unmistakable sound of Julia's excited voice echoing through the foyer.

Rachel heaved a sigh of relief. She wouldn't have to call in the Runners after all. Mr. Eastgate was a very fortunate gentleman.

Knowing that Julia would want to go to her room and rest after her outing, Rachel smoothed the skirts of her brilliant emerald gown.

She dearly loved her sisters and Julia, but she had neglected her poor husband long enough. She intended to rectify her oversight with all possible speed.

Moving across the room, Rachel quietly opened the door and closed it behind her.

For a moment she simply watched Anthony as he connected a series of gears that were to go into his latest invention. As always he had removed his cravat and coat and his dark hair was rumpled. A tide of love washed through her. Gads, how had she ever been so fortunate as to discover this man? Heaven certainly had smiled upon her.

Reaching behind her, Rachel turned the lock on the door, smiling as Anthony's head instantly lifted to regard her with anticipation.

Dropping his gears with satisfying swiftness, Anthony moved to stand before her.

"Have your sisters taken their leave?"

"Just now," she assured him.

"Ah." He slowly reached out to stroke the sensitive line of her neck. "Was there a special reason for their unexpected visit?"

"Yes, indeed. It appears I will soon have another brother or sister."

His brows lifted in surprise. "Egads."

"Quite shocking, is it not?"

He considered the matter for a moment before giving a wry smile.

"Considering we are speaking of the Devilish Dandy it is not so shocking as I might have feared."

She sent him a chiding frown then, was suddenly struck by inspiration.

"You know, Anthony, we shall have to make plans to travel to Italy. Violet will want to have someone she knows at hand when the baby is born. It will also be a wonderful opportunity for Julia to see something of the world."

Although Anthony gave a nod of his head, it was obvious his mind was not on her father, or even traveling to Italy. Instead his hands moved to begin plucking the pins from her curls until they tumbled about her shoulders in a riot of gold.

"Speaking of Julia, has she returned?"

"She arrived as my sisters were leaving," she murmured as her own thoughts became increasingly distracted.

"Good." Bending his head, he planted a series of tender kisses down the line of her jaw.

Rachel shivered, wrapping her arms around his neck.

"Sir, what are you doing?" she teased in uneven tones.

His hands moved to busy themselves with the ribbons that held her gown together.

"Now that you are no longer fretting over your missing chick, you are free to dwell upon your desperately lonely husband."

She sucked in a sharp breath as his warm hands found the skin of her back.

"I thought you were busy with your project?"

"Oh, I am," he promised in husky tones. "Indeed,

I have r—reached a most delicate stage. I am in great need of your expertise."

"As you know, I am always willing to share my expertise," she assured him as she arched closer.

He gave a husky chuckle as he easily swept her off her feet and carried her toward the distant sofa.

"Ah, my minx, I do love you."

"And I love you," she said, gazing deep into the dark eyes. "Forever and ever."

He slowly smiled, his gaze sweeping down to her parted lips.

"Now, about that project . . ."

ABOUT THE AUTHOR

Debbie Raleigh lives with her family in Missouri. She is currently working on her next Zebra Regency romance, the first of a new trilogy to be published in November 2002. Debbie loves to hear from readers and you may write to her c/o Zebra Books. Please include a self-addressed stamped envelope if you wish a response.

More Zebra Regency Romances

BOOK YOUR PLACE ON OUR WEBSITE AND MAKE THE READING CONNECTION!

We've created a customized website just for our very special readers, where you can get the inside scoop on everything that's going on with Zebra, Pinnacle and Kensington books.

When you come online, you'll have the exciting opportunity to:

- View covers of upcoming books
- Read sample chapters
- Learn about our future publishing schedule (listed by publication month *and author*)
- Find out when your favorite authors will be visiting a city near you
- Search for and order backlist books from our online catalog
- Check out author bios and background information
- Send e-mail to your favorite authors
- Meet the Kensington staff online
- Join us in weekly chats with authors, readers and other guests
- Get writing guidelines
- AND MUCH MORE!

**Visit our website at
http://www.kensingtonbooks.com**